Red Flour

Red Flour
A Novel

Seraj Assi

Philadelphia, PA
commonnotions.org

Red Flour: A Novel

ISBN: 978-1-945335-75-4 | eBook ISBN: 978-1-945335-89-1
Library of Congress Control Number: 2026948189

10 9 8 7 6 5 4 3 2 1

Common Notions
PO Box 18823
Philadelphia, PA 19119

commonnotions.org
info@commonnotions.org

Discounted bulk quantities of our books are available for organizing, educational, or fundraising purposes. Please contact Common Notions at the address above for more information.

Cover design by Josh MacPhee
Layout design and typesetting by Sydney Rainer
Printed on acid-free paper

About The Nonaligned Series

The Nonaligned Series is dedicated to fiction, literary nonfiction, and poetry that explores the historical and ongoing legacies of anticolonial politics, the evolving nature of imperialism, and the world-making freedom movements of our times. The series highlights vital and creative sources of internationalist imagination within the fractures and fault lines of the current world order. The name takes inspiration from the worldwide anticolonial and anti-imperialist self-determination movements that sparked a wave of decolonization in the 1960s and '70s across Africa, Latin America, Asia, and the Arab world.

Red Flour

Seraj Assi

To my little muse Sophia, who helped me write this book.

This is a book about witnessing a genocide, and worse still, surviving it.

—S.A.

Red Flour

Imagine my astonishment when I wake up from a long nightmare and find myself alive and breathing. In emotional tatters, but living still. You can tell that I'm alive from my wretched state, dreadful appearance, fast-graying hair, ghostlike face, and grief-stricken features. I also have recurrent nightmares and sudden spasms of rage and disgust, owing in great part to my lingering wounds and shrapnel-riddled body. My other scars are better left unseen.

My heart is beating, faintly but surely, and nothing says living like a beating heart. Broken, but beating, ticking eerily within, like a haunted clock chiming amid the rubble. I have a dim memory of being hungry, but I have lost the urge for food. I'm too stunned and numb to crave anything. I'm thirsty besides, but my thirst is unslakable, though a glass of cold water would do me good.

There is a certain agitation in my soul, a vestige of inexplicable horror, whose mere memory stalks my person like a permanent deformity. But my heart is pounding, slowly but firmly, like a time bomb left ticking. I nearly burst out weeping with nameless joy at still being alive—though I have a vague recollection of how and what I have survived. It looms in my memory like the residue of a bad dream. All I remember is a starving young man with a feeble will to survive. It was a night of mayhem. Or perhaps it was daytime. Or maybe twilight. I'm not sure. Memory blurs. Pain and hunger must've clouded my mind. The shock seems to have jolted my senses, for I can vaguely make things out. I remember there was a massive fusillade, like hell raining down, followed by chaos and great dispersion, scrambling and stumbling, and amid the panic and havoc, I passed into a red haze and was gone.

The rest is silence. Perhaps not completely silent, for I still hear voices in my head, a constant ringing in my ear, a restless whisper. I can hear the pale murmurs of my blood flowing. I feel strangely revived, raised from the dead, yet still slightly in pain, as if my saving angels had forgotten to remove the nails. I feel miraculously resurrected, yes, as if awakened by native incense, or aroused from a deep sleep by the aroma of freshly baked bread, whose ubiquitous fragrance is unmistakably present here. Its warm scent overwhelms my senses, and I'm not easily overwhelmed. It takes a miracle to stir me back to life after all I have witnessed. And if you witnessed the untold horror we lived, if you knew our story and heard our last howls on Earth, you would perhaps appreciate my miraculous resurrection, or at least understand what our people mean when they speak of the miracle of bread.

Allow me to elaborate while I can. In the local belief, bread making mimics the divine act of creation, where the marvel of breathing life into bread with flour and kneading is akin to creating life by blending dust and wind. My mother made bread that way; she was a goddess to her children. I remember her in the good old days, mixing flour and water into perfectly elastic dough, kneading it gently with her small hands. She watched the magic blend slowly rise and breathe as she fired up her stone oven while the creature rested. The result was perfect bread, which came out of the oven warm and soft, breathing still, gasping and panting like a child out of the womb. You should've seen her curling up by the fire, molding the dough, rolling it out, and gathering it up again, patting and coaxing it with grand flourish and flair! Dusting bread with flour. It was our daily miracle, wonderful while it lasted.

When that daily miracle is suspended, it means death. Except that death in this case is not divinely sanctioned, but human-made—carried out in the name of humanity. Humanity—a word I can hardly bear to utter without weeping with irony. Perhaps the greatest moral bombshell handed to us by this war is that there is no such thing as humanity; there are mortal spacemen known as human beings, who have yet to learn how to share a planet without tearing it to pieces.

So no, I'm not dead, for my heart is pulsing, feebly but surely, like the rising of homemade dough. I have a strange memory of myself gasping inside my mother's womb, her chest rising and sinking with heavy tides, screaming with joy as I kicked inside her like a prisoner beating on the bars, ready to spring into life, keen on the freedom I never had. I see a little tender thing, wrapped in a white blanket, blood still clinging to his small crimson body, gasping his first breaths while stirring slowly into life. He gazed on the world for the first time through his baffled, sleepy eyes, knowing little of life and all the madness and cruelty that awaited. Not knowing that he would depart this world in the same way he came, wrapped in a white coffin of spilled flour, soaked red with his own blood, and little else.

It's startling to think that I can remember the particulars of my birth and my death, but little in between. I can conjure my mother, yes, but only vaguely, and in fragments. I recollect there was a girl, a beautiful young girl, but I'm not quite able to make out her face or conjure up her memory. However, I do recall that she bore an uncanny resemblance to my mother. But who she was, and what became of her—I can no longer tell. She dwells in my memory as a vague yet pervasive wound.

I see a breadline forming in the bloody hours of dawn, followed by great chaos and bloodshed, and multitudes of vultures and dogs coming to feast on the carnage, but I'm blanking on the rest, as if a wicked magician had thrown a blanket over my memory and left me in the dark. Perhaps I'm too anguished to remember. Or perhaps I have lost my memory for good. Perhaps if I let myself rest and unwind a little, my memories will ultimately resurface, and I shall slowly find my feet and gather my wits. Or perhaps I'm dead and bereft of memory, which could be a blessing when you think of it.

I look around and see a place like no other. It bears a vague resemblance to my dear old hometown, which no longer exists, or perhaps exists only as a shell of its former glory. How else would you explain the eerie presence of blood oranges and ghostly olive trees, and these haunting pines that seem older than the soil in which they stand? I make out a river, flowing into busy streams and watering the golden wheat fields, which sail into my line of vision like undulating waves. It must be springtime, for I can hear birds singing nearby, see the flowers drifting in the gentle wind, and smell the scent of freshly baked bread. Their wafting aroma awakens my senses as if by magic, flying on invisible wings. A sudden craving overtakes me, and my belly growls and rumbles in its own great emptiness, and I suddenly realize that I haven't tasted food for a long while. I hardly remember when was the last time I had something to eat. I recall, shortly before I passed out, a rescuer was offering me something to eat to save myself, or perhaps to die content and untortured, but I was too nauseated by the sight of bloodshed to accept it. The place was waist-deep in blood, teeming with the foul reek of death, and filling the very air we breathed like a hot red simoom. I was so sick and disgusted that there was nothing I could possibly cherish more than hunger. I was sad and heartbroken, and my sorrow was inconsolable by food. There was a child, a bone-thin boy, dashing madly about with his bowl of flour. Blood was oozing from his face—weeping, screaming, jockeying for safety under a relentless barrage of fire—before he fell to the ground, lifeless, his face a blend of white and red. That was the last thing I remember seeing before I passed out. The sight chilled the very marrow of my bones. My heart dropped, my blood ran cold, and I went out in a blur. It was hard to tell whether I was dead or alive, or a living dead, but it hardly mattered; there was nothing left to live for, or die for, nothing but a land red with mad martyrdom.

Yet here I am breathing still, my heart beating like the faint murmur of subsiding rain. Of the violence I witnessed and sustained, there is but a pale residue of red scars, which seem to heal like an enchantment, as if cured by a divine touch. It's as if a magician had poured pixie powder on my wounds. What right do I have to be alive when many of my kind perished? And how can I be sure, absolutely sure, that I'm still alive? At least I'm not dead, if by dead you mean the cessation of a heartbeat. What a fathomless mystery the human heart is! Death overtakes you, and it keeps beating within, like a survivor under the rubble. I'm alive to my good fortune, yes. I'm safe and sound, and well out of harm's way. My skin is still on me. My body is almost intact, in one piece. Surely, you've heard of the rescuer who bursts into happy tears when he discovers that his own child, long missing under the rubble, is alive, in tatters, but breathing still, then proceeds quietly and without much ado to stitch his child back together? Besides the shrapnel that has perforated my skin, I'm perfectly whole. I still have my hands and legs, unshredded by a dumb bomb.

It's my heart that's bleeding. Yet I'm alive, yes. What is a more telling sign of life than an aching heart? The rest is mere cosmetics. A dusty brown powder has settled on my clothes. It could be dust or flour still clinging to my person. My hair looks as if dipped in flour, but when I try to dust it off, it does not clear out, so I assume it's just the token of extreme anguish, owing likely to the sheer horror I witnessed on Earth—though I can still smile. I even laugh with sardonic irony at still being alive, which you would appreciate had you been there.

I take a moment to wonder by what inexplicable miracle I have wound up in this heavenly place that resembles no other. No, I was not abducted by aliens and beamed away on a flying saucer. If I feel weightless, it's only because I departed our mother Earth hungry. If I feel stranded in a time warp, it's merely because I'm still hallucinating from hunger. Neither was I saved by angels, nor resurrected by divine powers, though having witnessed the past and its horrors, the present holds no surprises for me. As my people say, nothing is too far-fetched.

On closer inspection, I feel like I have landed on the moon. This feeling takes hold of me whenever I gaze down on the ruins of my hometown, which truly resembles an otherworldly landscape, space dust covering the rubble.

Dusting the flour off, I rise and walk about the place like a newly-awakened ghost, fresh out of the grave. I lend my ears to the echoing silence, and what do I hear but the first stirrings of human life! I see a child, smiling heartily through his chubby cheeks and full mouth. He stands there shoving bread in his mouth as if breaking a fast. "I was a skeleton once," he tells me, while taking in a big mouthful. His eerie joke rattles me. But he seems happy, comfortable in his fat frame. He appears determined to put on more weight, to be twice as fat, as if still haunted by the prospect of hunger. His insatiable appetite bears the impression of someone who starved before. He says I look like a zombie, and, glimpsing myself in my mental mirror, I smile at the image. He offers me a slice of bread, which I accept gratefully. I ask him about a girl—freckled face, olive eyes, strong features—and he points to a group of girls gathered nearby. They're dipping bread in what looks like a river of red jam, and I consider whether I am hallucinating. My mind, which seems to retain memories of extreme hunger and hallucinations, feels like a desert. I still feel a certain pain, a permanent emptiness in my belly, a trace of desolate memories. I see things, fancy things, but I have little faith in my senses. One moment, an image passes before my eyes; the next, it vanishes into thin air. I feel stranded in existential limbo. I could be dead or alive, all the same.

But the child seems real. There he sits unperturbed, chewing his bread with the smug contentment of someone who suffered so much on Earth and is finally rewarded.

His unholy munching noises, which once annoyed me on Earth, are now my only reminder of being alive. But surely this heavenly bread tastes real—it smells good. I hardly remember the last time I tasted something so delightful. It's so delicious it can be eaten plain and dry. My poor parents always made the case that bread could be eaten by itself, especially when the house was fresh out of butter and jam, which was often. But the bread was palatable in those days. Baked with love and plenty of flour for a rich flavor with soft textures—a truly wholesome delight. It was to die for, if only we knew it!

I thank the boy for the bread, and he smiles and hands me a piece of flatbread, baked to perfection—not too chewy, not too crispy, earthly, and slathered with olive oil, which he says one can only find in these parts of heaven. The bread tastes so familiar that a mere bite brings back a flood of memories. I see my mother curled up by her old stone oven, her dark face red from the reflection of flames, sweat rolling freely down her flaming cheeks, as if sunbathing.

"Are you here alone?" he asks me, still munching his bread. His question startles me, for when I hark back to my last moments on Earth, I remember feeling extremely lonely, like the sole survivor of a people now dead. There was a girl in my life, if you must know—or more precisely, a girl who gave me a reason to live, for I was the walking dead then.

There was a girl—what was her name? There was a girl, a nameless girl, whose beauty and bravery offered me hope and purpose amid all that despair. We barely exchanged a word—it was all in the eyes, and if you had seen her eyes, you would've appreciated their speechless beauty. A pair of pale-green oases, like two olive groves gleaming in the early dawn.

We made a promise, a nonverbal one, to stay alive—but one of us broke it. No, it *was* broken, born dead—a broken promise, made in a broken place, in broken times. For how can love possibly blossom and prosper in a place ravaged by hunger, where no romance can flourish, and the only red roses are painted with blood? Love in a breadline, what a farce! And yet we fell for it, yes, for we were human, all too human. We succumbed to it like two desert wanderers standing before a mirage and swearing it's an oasis. You may resist an occupier, you may resist an invading power, you may resist an overwhelming force, but there's no resisting love, for it disarms us and leaves us utterly defenseless before we know it. We feel powerless in its presence, but we accept our defeat, yes; we embrace our fall and gladly surrender ourselves to its powers. It occupies us, and we still greet it with flowers! What a farce love is, what a mad affair! You see two wretched souls, starving to death, yet dreaming of red roses while the earth under their feet burns.

It's still night here, and the moon is out in its full glory. In the dead of night, I remember her—oh, night, making all things dimly beautiful and vividly sad! I remember two souls gazing out on the road, dreaming of love and freedom—two starving bodies, a pair of desolate yet loving hearts beating in unison in a desert of utter destitution where nothing else bloomed. In the dead of night, her freckled face comes alive, like a vivid midsummer daydream, and with it the memory of our unfulfilled promise, a promise sealed in blood and upended only by death. *Why did I abandon her?* What does a pudgy little boy with a face like a loaf know about life and death—or love? Do you think I did not wish to take her in my arms and show her the red roses in the sky? Do you think I did not wish to shield her with my bare body, *save* her, and die the death of a martyr? Take her in my arms and walk her to safety? It was total chaos, and all I could see were dark skies and a ground soaked in red and white. It happened in a blur and ended with a bloodbath. What was I to do? I was starving, wounded, bleeding. I hardly had enough strength left to pick up a shovel and dig a grave. There was no time for mourning or goodbyes. Do you understand that?

The encounter has left me vaguely unsettled. Stirred back to life, I begin to slowly regain my memory. I have seen this child before, in his skeletal phase, and all the chubby children who have now gathered around him, munching their bread like famished cubs. I can hardly remember the last time I saw a healthy kid in these quarters. Surely the rascals have some fat to burn! When I was a schoolboy, there was a chubby kid in our class whom we tantalized daily, believing he was overeating. When starvation devoured the camp, the poor lad was among the first to go. They say his grave was smaller than his cradle.

I smile with irony as I reflect on those worldly events, now I'm saved, full, and content. It gives me thrills to see the children, who perished from starvation, fattening themselves on this heavenly bread—eternally fresh and never stale—it bakes itself, as if by magic. It comes to you by merely wishing for it! There is an infinite selection of spreads: chocolate, jam, butter, and honey. It amazes me to see that the olive oil spread of the dear old homeland remains untouched. But one is free to eat whatever one pleases in heaven. And those who starved our children on Earth and gloated in their torment? They are in hell, of course, where a strange punishment is meted out to them: they are made to starve, and then offered bread, plenty of it, but whenever they venture to eat it, it burns instantly into ashes. The children call it divine justice, and they firmly believe in it, for it would be inhumane to believe otherwise. Who's gloating now? Yes, gloating, and quite triumphantly so! Why shouldn't I gloat? I would ululate if I knew how. For that's how our people imagine heaven: A place where the oppressed can finally have their moment under the sun, and rejoice, yes, rejoice over the fate of their earthly tormentors.

The children then start a playful skirmish, boasting over who can eat more and gain still more weight, before embarking, for the sheer fun of it, on a lively food contest—a game in which only the fattest win. It's like a hunger game in reverse. I watch with awed admiration as they wolf down the food in earnest. They seem to revel in the fare. Look at them, smiling through full mouths and swollen cheeks, filled with food on either side, and seeming so puffy you wonder how the lovable rascals breathe! Cheers erupt as the winner, the boy with the chubby cheeks, receives a velvet cake made of red flour. Almost instantly, he dips his round head in it with crimson energy, his face waxing so red from the cake, it lends him the resemblance of a bomb survivor. The spectacle evokes strange emotions in me. Having witnessed it all, I burst into a violent spasm of ironic laughter and nearly bust a gut. It's truly the first laughter I have managed in a long time.

So, I'm not dead, or at least that's what the red tracks on my face tell me. I can taste blood in my mouth, like the sour tang of death. In a place where even the air is dead, blood is a sign of life. The boy was right, I do look like a zombie, except I do not feed on human flesh nor eat human brains—perhaps this explains why I let myself starve to death when I could, heaven forbid, eat my own flesh! Our land was littered with dead human meat that offered itself in plenty to those who were too tormented by hunger to bother with taboos. It sat on the road unheeded, rotting away, exhorting us with its forbidden allure like the dark glint of despair—a last stab at life, or perhaps a dreadful spew in the face of death. But I was never afraid of death. I have met the grim monster so many times in this hellscape I hardly ever tremble in its presence. There are people on this sad Earth to whom death is not the worst of destinies. It may indeed prove kinder to them than life, and there may even come times when nothing kinder could be imagined. What's the worst that can befall us here? Death, resting in peace. We call that *kismet*. If there's heaven, God bless. Otherwise, we have escaped this hell, and that's heaven enough. And yet there's no escaping the thought that death might not be the end of our misery, only the beginning of some eternal suffering. For what if your last feeling at the moment of death accompanies you to the grave? And what if that last feeling was hunger? A lasting hunger, how torturesome! Or what if you died thirsty and found death unsatiating? What an eternal nightmare it would be to thirst infinitely in these parched quarters!

No, I'm not afraid of death. I'm just mortified to be alive while many of my kind perished; it's no consolation to find yourself the last survivor of a people now dead. It's hard enough to outlive a loved one; imagine a whole nation! Fate is a strange thing; for more than we wish to admit, there is more luck than heroism in survival. People like to think that fate is the residue of some divine intervention. But it's truly blind, and there is nothing divine about it. So, what right have I to survive what killed many others, when death was so rife, and there were so many eyes to shut, but few hands to do it? I'm not a hero. If I survived—which remains doubtful, for it takes more than heartbeats to convince me that I'm not dead and hallucinating—if I survived, it's only because I had acquired, war after war, certain survival qualities, which are more instinctive than divine. I was like a cat that senses danger by deploying its God-given senses. Or perhaps a rat that seeks cover when hell rains down, and ventures out when the rain stops, and the sky beams with a rainbow.

I was no hero; I too threw my empty bowl into the dust and fled for dear life when hell rained down. I'm not a hero because there *are* no heroes in this world, only wolves and lambs. The lamb may survive and even resist the wolf, but that would only incite the wolf and turn it into a monster. That's human history in tragic miniature. I remember one holiday, my devoted father was about to sacrifice a small offering to please his God, but it was a stubborn young animal, a highly dignified one that put on a rare show of resistance. Perhaps the sheep, in his vainglorious ecstasy, merely wanted to impress the ewes. Or perhaps it was a proud beast that saw no dignity in being herded to the altar without so much as resistance—a lamb who refused to be sheeplike. I was all in awe of the poor creature, but my father was incensed. "Meat does not grow on trees, my son," he would say, mocking my childish protests. There was a brief comic skirmish, then knives came out, followed by slaughter, and the inevitable silence of the lamb. I wept for the poor little woolly, and chided my father for it, not knowing that one day my father himself would be the offering.

But there was one hero, yes, if by hero you mean a lamb that refuses to be cowed. I never learned her name, for the real heroes in this world often go nameless. She was standing in the designated food line, holding her empty bowl and gazing at a mound of flour sacks. When the soldiers fired the first shots, she did not budge an inch. She merely stood there with astonishing resilience, foolish but startling, determined to leave with her promised bowl of flour, as if saying to the soldiers that she would rather perish by the bullets than die hungry. Was she a hero? Perhaps more of a stubborn one than a hero—a dignified lamb. Oh, dignity, for shame, how many beautiful souls have we sacrificed in your name! When you are starved to death, when you are reduced to your primal needs, you do not see the world in terms of heroism or mad martyrdom; you simply follow your instincts in the heat of the moment. But if you happen to be a member of a madly dignified people, then you have it in your genes, and there's no helping it, for you were born into it, doomed, *condemned* to it. I never learned her name, and perhaps never will, and now she's gone. But her image, her freckled face, olive eyes, and her strong features will always haunt me like a spirit. And it haunts me even more to think that even to her one and only lover, she died nameless, as if she was never born. But I was not a coward. If I did not take her on my white steed and fly her to safety, it's only because the horses had already perished from hunger. And if the mighty horses perished, imagine the fate of the lambs?

How did it all happen? I have a faint recollection of it. The pain must've dulled my memory. I remember it was sunshine. Or maybe sunset. It's hard to tell, for the place was so submerged in red, I went nearly colorblind. I still hear the howls, the sad lamentations, the roaring fires. It was hell on Earth, which for most people is just an expression. The tender souls who perished from hunger, who died waiting with their empty bowls and emaciated bodies, I remember them all. They were standing there, casting empty glances toward the gates, gazing out through hollowed eyes, wondering for what sin they were being starved. Then the bullets rained down, and in an instant, they were gone, vanished like dust, a moment too short for them to wonder for what unspeakable sin they were murdered. They must be in heaven right now. Or so we believe, for we would go mad if we believed otherwise. Perhaps death *is* heaven, the prospect of escaping hell on Earth, where nothing breathes but the dust of our rubble.

It's not far-fetched. I can hear children laughing and playing in the vicinity, sounding happy and content. I can hear the soft whispers of my mother, and father, and brothers, and sister, and all the loved ones who died waiting for the flour that never came. I can see my grandmother, baking heavenly bread that never ages, her stone mill running tirelessly like a spinning cotton yarn. I fancy my sweetheart, wearing a spotless white dress, smiling and laughing to herself without an inkling of the tragedy that befell her on Earth. Red roses have bloomed in place of the gory bloodstains that once marked her tragic death. Even the poor animals are here, basking in eternal peace. Who said there were no dogs in heaven? I might be hallucinating, but the image persists and takes hold of my mind—it's too hard to dislodge. So, it *must* be heaven, or at least some version of it. It's not perfect, for I still have my memories, but it's heaven still. Perhaps it's not heaven, merely a respite from the hell thereunder. For the truth is that evil will always prevail on Earth, and all we can do is mollify it some, or perhaps defy it by means of fantastical escapism and lofty promises of divine justice and eternal happiness.

Or perhaps the war has ended, which is hard to swallow. For war here never ends, only puts on new faces, each uglier than the last. They say we hardly need another war to understand that history repeats itself, but since history repeats itself, the next war is coming. It's unfolding as we speak, roaring for our blood. There will always be war, so long as nations continue to exist on this Earth, and humans crave power and craft lofty slogans to beautify their crimes. They cloak their inevitable mortality with false promises of glory, though if they wait a bit longer, they will all die eventually. But human vanity is too vast and deep to fathom, and people will always fight, and find a reason for it—if not for a flimsy cause, then for the sheer fun of it—fighting for its own sake. Fighting for sport. It's humanity's pastime. And if they find no weaker nation to fight and throw against the wall and turn into hooked meat, they would fight among themselves. A brother's war, they call it. It's in their genes, sown in the very genesis of humanity, which, little surprise, started with a murder.

There will always be wars, more wars, and still other wars. But what happened here bears almost no resemblance to what historians call war. There's nothing noble about it. There is no glory, no dignity, no victory, and no heroes. It's a new sort of evil, a novel yet vile manifestation of cruelty, a depravity we never knew existed. And if you never believed in human evil, if you believe the designation is obsolete and outmoded, too antiquated and archaic, and beneath your intellectual or secular dignity, a short walk down our valley of death will likely convert you. For what happened here has no precedent in the chronicles of nations. Historians still have no word for it, and perhaps never will, for no words can contain the horror that unfolded in this doomed place. I will tell you how it all unfolded, now that I'm resurrected and have eternity on my hands to reflect, ponder, and marvel at the sheer paradox of human justice. If you happen to believe in historical justice, just remember that in a thousand years or so, this horror will become the stuff of tragicomic laughter, if remembered at all. For human memory is too short and ephemeral to retain a tragedy of this magnitude without bleaching the horror out of it.

One needs a fair dose of imagination to take that vatic leap into the future and understand that historical justice is nothing but an opium, a sugar pill to console the oppressed who never knew peace on this Earth—that historical reckoning is meant only for those who can write and rewrite history. And what good is historical justice for a people now dead, who are no longer alive to enjoy this belated redemption and reap its fruits? And where was that justice when we wanted it, when we screamed and pleaded for it? I will tell you how it all unfolded, if you promise to spare me your smug philosophical apathy toward human suffering. If you promise to suspend your lofty detachment and tear down that fourth wall that separates you from our suffering and give our tale the dignity it deserves. But first, allow me to register my utter horror and contempt for all things human. For the horror we witnessed here has rendered bright the darkest chapters of humanity. Future historians will scratch their heads over how it was allowed to happen. I can hear them howling back at our age of shame with cosmic, tragic laughter, busting their guts over the myth of our time—the belief in a shared humanity. They will laugh at it and find no one to stop them.

Perhaps one day the poets of the world will compose odes to our saga. Perhaps when the dust settles and the blood clears, a new chapter of humanity will be written. We will put those human monsters in it, and it won't be flattering. But I'm not deluded, for history will not tell the tragedies enacted here without allowing time to intervene in great measure to assuage and lend an azure tint to them—for what is dark humor but tragedy plus time? As my history teacher liked to say, "Tragedy is like flour; it tends to bleach with time." Now imagine a tragedy whose very threads are woven out from the deprivation of flour.

It was wartime, and as always happens in wartime, people were starving—or *starved,* to be more precise. You will be amazed at how these things can be twisted by the sheer manipulation of grammar. The number of crimes that can be buried under layers of semantics, where human agency often gets lost in translation, and all that evil will be blamed squarely on a natural disaster or an act of God. It was wartime, and people were *forcibly* starved, roaming the streets with growling bellies, empty pots, and the gauntest bodies to ever walk this Earth. One felt like walking in a land of zombies, with the living dead collapsing in the streets from hunger and exhaustion. It was harrowing to witness, but it happened so often it was impossible not to witness. I myself fainted so often, I felt like sleepwalking into a liminal existence, or a dreamless nightmare. Every time I came to, I felt as if I returned from the dead, resurrected but not saved, which was a torment when you think about it. The camp was gazing down the abyss, and when mayhem happened, there was no hell beyond that. There were no deeper depths to plumb, and no threshold left to cross. It was hell all the way down. Yes, massacres are boring. I know, I know! There is nothing interesting to say about a massacre, for everyone is supposed to be dead, and everything is supposed to be very quiet afterward, but we must not give in to the temptation of complacency. Yes, evil can be gloomy, boring and barren, a sheer monotony, but so is hell. And no, I'm not asking for your sympathy, or empathy, not for want of gratitude, but simply because the victims are no longer here to appreciate it.

It was a day like no other, so dark and full of melancholy the sun refused to come out. In hindsight, this is baffling. A rainbow was about to appear in the sky and usher in joy; the children had made their kites and kept them unfolded in anticipation of playing. The stone ovens were set, the fire built, and the flour bowls waiting for the old women, ready to work magic and bring to life the daily miracle of bread. And in the secret of that euphoria, love was blooming, and two yearning souls in the full spring of youth were about to witness the first stirrings of desire—as if something plain had quietly started to bloom in vivid reds. Surely there were other lovers, and more loves flourishing, but this particular romance was too powerful to be upended by sheer force, or so I fancied. And even now, I still marvel at how a force so great and overwhelming that it rivals destiny itself can be shattered in just a moment, leaving hardly a trace. But I'm more relaxed now, fully disenchanted, and sober enough to understand that the inventory of people's passions and desires, hopes and dreams, can barely withstand the destructive force of a dumb bomb unleashed to gratify the pride and vanity of a handful of war-loving generals.

One day was all it took me to comprehend this grim human reality. Everything changed that day, and all that was good and noble melted into thin air. For example, we had thought red was the color of love, only to discover, to our collective shock and disgust, that love was a colorless mirage—excuse me if I laugh, but the irony is too dark to resist. We know now that red has but one shade, and it's not a pleasant one. It reeks of death and decay, and it's too dreadful to bear. And to think that before that day

I was queasy about blood, that I was nauseated by the mere sight of it, that I would faint at the sheer prospect of drawing blood from my veins! Will these laughable ironies ever end? Blood was ubiquitous, too common and mundane to register on the eyes. If you listen closely, you could hear it cry from the ground! It rumbled on the surface and visibly beneath it. The land was drenched waist-deep in sickening warmth, red with the blood of my people. We have always had wars here. But this one was extraordinary.

This war produced more horrors and misery than all other wars in the annals of our people. We have had our fair share of those, but none nearly as horrific as the one that unfolded that day. For that day was not another day in hell; it *was* hell. It dwarfs all the horrors I have read in history books, and I have read plenty. My father had a huge library, before it burned down, which mainly consisted of history books, and a hundred copies of one sacred book. My father believed humans should learn from history, lest they repeat it—excuse me for laughing again, but it seems this heaven is having a soothing effect on me. We are a merry people; that's how we fool tragedy. We either laugh or perish from despair. I was saying it was a new kind of horror, a horror we never knew existed. It defies fiction and puts to shame the entire Gothic canon. It renders comical the finest tragedies of the old Greeks. Believe me, having lived real life and its horrors, fiction holds no terror for me. I have looked in vain in the annals of nations for a fate of this kind. It makes you feel quite special, being the victim of the worst crime committed by the human race—perhaps not the worst, but surely the vilest and most dishonorable. And that's the only instance you are allowed to feel that way. For the most part, you are a cockroach that scurries whenever the light shines on it, a mortal thing clinging hopelessly to the dead surface. If you survive, good for you. If you perish, the world will probably take no notice.

The story might sound incredible, but you must remember that it occurred at a time in human history when slaying people who were simply waiting for flour hardly caused a global shrug. For the world looked away that day. I remember when I was a child, I read a short story about a hunger artist who locks himself in a cage and starves himself to death in the vainglorious pursuit of fame, yet to his malice, the public gaze slowly turns away from him. That's precisely what happened to us here, except that we are real human beings, made of flesh and blood, and not invented characters in a piece of fiction. Now, try to explain the art of starving to someone from this century! Those who have no feel for it can never be made to understand it. If you fast, if you starve yourself to experience hunger, for whatever spiritual or artistic reason, that's your choice. But when you are *forcibly* starved, then it's a death sentence, meted out to you by people who have no right to seal your fate or condemn you to that kind of death. But they did it, and celebrated it, and they found no one among them to condemn it.

Now to our story.

Red Flour

It's an early spring day, though this is impossible to tell from the weather, for seasons have long ceased to exist here, thanks to the incessant bombing. All the usual signs that herald spring are sadly absent: There are no flowers blooming, nor birds chirping, nor sheep grazing on the meadows, nor joyful cries of the newborn lambs. One can hardly tell day from night in this timeless hellscape. So often the unceasing bombing collapses night into day, although sometimes, when the smoke of war engulfs the sky, it waxes so dark I wonder if the sun has been blotted out for good. It so happens that the delirious children mistake a blast for a sunrise. Many tender souls have perished while chasing the sun or the moonlight. So often the massive bombs cause rainbows to appear in the sky, and the kids would gather down there to admire the celestial view, wondering whether the war had ended or started. For long, hellish months, the poor souls have waited for the colorful wonder to emerge in the sky and usher in peace, which never did come. Nothing ever comes but death and more death. One is lucky to merely survive, though the prospect of survival seems to diminish with each passing hour. Sometimes I can't figure out what I have survived—as everything dear and beautiful I knew here has been destroyed. People, animals, trees. Even the little scarecrows have been crucified on their crosses, which hardly matters, for the wheat fields had burned down, and the birds have taken flight. The landscape is but scorched earth, and the ashen soil yields nothing but dark vegetation. The land is gorged with rubble, resembling a body that has decomposed save for the bones. But you hold on to life, if only to defy death. It amazes me how people cling so firmly to life where life itself has ceased to exist. It's baffling, but human. Everything has been destroyed, and we still long for something to eat, a piece of bread to put out the fires within.

No, there was no rainbow, and even if there was one, our hallucinating children would likely misconstrue it as a confetti cake, or fruit salad, or veggie pizza. Or perhaps one of those colorful ice-cream popsicles that once delighted our little hearts and soothed our summers of discontent. I was a child crazy about rainbows. I awaited them like an old prophet anticipating a heavenly omen. As luck would have it, my father had an inherent fear of displacement, and he kept a telescope to look out for human invaders at sea, not realizing that the new invaders were falling upon us from the sky. He also kept a clock, which kept time, and it was a good time to keep, if only we knew it! He hoarded food for a rainy day, which we squandered in our bemusement, thinking it would never rain in this wasteland, unaware that when heaven and Earth pull apart, and hell rains down, there will be nothing left to shore against our ruin but fragments of uneaten food our fathers had left us in their perceptive vigilance.

There was no rainbow, and there was never going to be one. Even when our blood cloaks the streets, when the blood-drenched earth rolls together like a mighty red carpet for the marching soldiers, the rain does not bother to come down. But today, at last, the rainbow seems in sight, for it appears to us that we have survived the flood, and endured the hunger, and are soon to be saved. In our hopeful desperation, we have embraced the divine logic of the sacred books of yore, where humans suffered, and endured, and then the heart of providence softened and showered mercy on Earth. We believe it, and what do we have but faith? For the truth is that we would go insane if we did not cling to that belief, though when things fall apart, even that last bulwark against madness falls.

The red sun indicates early morning, or the bloody hours of dawn, to be more precise. The breadline has been forming all night long, ever since the flour rumors—the welcome news of aid trucks loaded with flour and heading our way—started to travel through the besieged camps at the speed of fire. Flour, that magic substance that makes life possible! Thousands of years have passed, and it has never lost its power to mete out life and death on this land! For hours, children, women, and old men, with empty bowls and empty bellies, have stood here waiting, casting hopeful gazes toward the horizon. The children resemble skeletons. They haven't seen bread for days. They look delirious with hunger and exhaustion. They have those lifeless eyes, hollowed and sunken cheeks, and the saddest faces I have ever seen. They seem not able to understand for what sin they are being deprived of the most primordial substance necessary to sustain life.

In their delirious state, they will tell you that God created humans from flour. They will tell you God Himself is made of flour, that He is the bread of life. They will tell you stories of ancient people who took their dough in haste before it was leavened, their kneading troughs bound up in clothes upon their shoulders. They will tell tales of ancient prophets who traveled to Egypt for grains, so that their people may live and not die. Give us food; now, why should we die before you?

"It's hard to believe these monsters were children once," an old man screams through the crowd. He strikes me as someone who has lost faith in humankind. His words rattle me to the core. I wish I could have a word with our besiegers and dare them to look at our bone-thin children. Can you face these children, look them straight in the eye, and tell them by what human logic, what divine law, they are being starved? No, you can't, because if you do, then there's something wrong with your humanity. Instead, you kill them from a distance, from afar, bomb them from the air, or shoot them indiscriminately, or kill them with the invisible weapon of starvation. But you never look them straight in the eye. I dare you to look them straight in the eye! Do you know what it means to watch your children starve to death before your eyes while you sit there helpless, doing nothing, for nothing you could do would soothe the burning fires within?

"Do you have children?" a woman, holding a pair of gaunt children in either hand, screams at the soldiers who stand guarding the gates with smug smiles on their unperturbed faces. I find myself wrestling with her question, though it's clearly not directed to me. An imaginary encounter unfolds in my mind as I subject the soldiers to one of my moral tirades, which is quite astonishing given my debilitated state of mind. Do you have children? I'm asking you; don't look away! Yes, you—do you have children? I bet you don't. Or perhaps, if you do, you believe that your children are made from nobler elements, and that the world would make less sense, indeed become less livable, less fair and just, if *your* young ones suffered. Surely you believe your children are made of light, and those of other people are made of darkness. Or perhaps you believe our little ones are not fully human, that they are subhuman, or maybe human animals, for it would be impossible for you to starve our children if you deemed them equally human.

Sometimes, when despair takes hold of me, I imagine myself in possession of some supernatural power, a superhuman thing flapping my magical wings and flying over the besieged town to deliver food and relief to the hungry. Like the ancient god who stole the secret of fire and divulged it to humanity. Or parting the deep blue sea with my magic staff to let my people pass to a kinder place, a land of plenty where food is abundant, and flour never runs out. I see myself in a free land, a land without gates, or walls, or borders, or tunnels, or landmines. A land without rubble, a land without bombs, or rockets, or drones, a land where the only cannons firing are those marking the end of a daily fast, a land—

My reverie is cut short by the renewed bombing nearby. It amazes me—and I'm not easily amazed, having witnessed more miracles on this land than heaven could ever produce—that for all the bombing, people here remain determined to keep their place in the flour queue. They're like condemned prisoners on death row, hoping to be granted their collective last wish. However, we have never experienced anything resembling justice, if justice ever existed on this Earth. But there they are, standing in the line, clinging to their empty bowls, casting their empty gazes upon the gates, and feeding their hearts on hopeful reveries. You see a child, bone-thin and battered by hunger and exhaustion, tilting like a branch blowing in the wind, clinging bravely to his bowl, while his feeble body threatens to collapse under him. It's hard to know what goes on in his head. Most likely, his mind has gone blank, blacked out, lost in the empty desert of deprivation. He's been standing in this torturous way for hours, bearing the eerie resemblance of a scarecrow, saying nothing, for his throat is probably too dry to speak. And even if he could speak, words would likely die on his parched little lips, which are showing fissures like a land in the throes of a drought. I have also noticed that his eyes are constantly shut, which I attribute to daydreaming. Or maybe hallucinating. For a fleeting moment, I imagined that he died standing. It's not wholly inconceivable, for I have noticed that in matters of life and death, our people tend to take after the old native trees of this land, which die standing. These steadfast trees have indestructible roots, and so when they die, the roots live on. Where do you suppose we learned to scurry underground when death looms?

Red Flour

Hunger is a heartless beast that eats at you slowly but surely. It devours you and burns inside you like fire. I know because I have been starving for days, hallucinating like a desert nomad who fancies an oasis where nothing breathes but deadly air and dust. I miss bread. I long for a last bite of it. I yearn for a last chance to smell it, touch it, feel its warmth in my mouth. Let that be my last wish. Give me a piece of bread and a cup full of fresh nectar from those homegrown oranges to wash it down. For this scorching heat is too oppressive for bread to swallow alone. Give me a basket full of flour, and watch the magic of creation unfold, for if there is anything our earthbound people excel in, it's breadmaking.

I dream of my late mother, baking bread in the old stone oven, its aroma so sweet I could devour it in the air. Visions of ancient swallows sail into the empty spaces of my deprivation. Memories of food roam freely in my parched mind, images of homemade delicacies that once abounded here, like a silhouette of a lost paradise, a paradise whose skies were the color of hell-flames, but a paradise still. I remember myself tearing at the bread as it came out of the oven, sizzling hot, burning my fingers in the process. I remember a hungry little rascal, standing too close to the glowing oven, his face nearly on fire, red glow flaming up in his cheeks. It was happiness and contentment in disguise. I remember a boy in the happiness of childhood, walking barefoot from the local bakery, a loaf of freshly baked bread tucked deftly under his arm, joy writ large on his tender face. It was a peaceful time to live, if only we knew it!

That's just a memory now. Last time I saw the bakery, it was teeming with hungry kids rummaging for burned crumbs in the ashes, heedless of warnings that a second bomb was hovering over the bakery that would spare nothing. For there is always a second bomb, and a third, and more if the place still shows life. Flour has been depleted with hardly a trace, and the only bread available is the one we dream up in our starved imagination, and good luck dreaming on an empty stomach! They say man shall not live by bread alone. Imagine when bread becomes a memory! I remember the wheat in the fields sailing freely in the golden sunshine, tilting in the gentle wind, dancing to the rhythms of nature. When milled into flour, it made a salty flavor, owing to their proximity to the sea, whose breeze never failed to deliver. Then bombs dropped, and the music stopped, and the fields burned to ashes, to starve us, or perhaps condemn us to a slow, agonizing death.

Bread is revered here. The greatest sin imaginable is not murder, but throwing away bread, because when you throw away bread, you desecrate life itself. You will anger the gods who provide it, and the earth that yields it, and please the evil forces that will seize on the first chance to see you starve to death and gloat over your misfortune. If a piece of bread drops on the ground, you must pick it up, kiss it, and thank heaven for it. And when you break it at a meal, you must do it with the utmost gentleness, tenderly and gratefully, as if tearing a page. We broke bread the way our father leafed through his sacred book—so reverently, lest he damage its spine.

"But if bread is sacred, then why doesn't it rain flour?" I was presented with this philosophical question by a kid, an extremely starved kid, whose body had withered into a frightful shell, and his skin hung in grotesque folds on his emaciated frame, threatening to fall off. "And if humans were made in God's image, then why do we starve and go hungry?" he ponders, not waiting for my answer, for I have none, and he knows it. It's astounding that a creature so feeble and frail, and kept alive by a miracle, can still harbor such complex thoughts, which perhaps proves my theory that hunger and its hallucinations give flight to the imagination. And we *are* imaginative people, a race of hopeless dreamers always hallucinating beyond life itself. A rich vein of optimism runs in our blood. There is no ceiling, no roof to our visions, only that illimitable space that hatched our first ancestors.

Our hopes get us by, our visions sustain us, and our dreams keep us standing. No matter what the future holds in store for us, we look to it with blazing eyes and burning hearts. Once a vision has taken hold and has us in its grip, it becomes impossible to dislodge. Come war or death, we never quit. Many of us die dreaming. We believe death is the beginning of a life of eternal happiness and absolute goodness. Fantasy is embedded in our genes. We indulge in it constantly, building castles in heaven where beautiful angels in white gowns wait to usher us into a life of everlasting pleasure. We are hooked on the afterlife, delirious at the prospect of our own death. Starve us, and we will feed our hearts on promises of rivers of milk and honey.

Perhaps it's the climate, or the sheer grind of life under siege, or maybe the unending war and all its miseries. We have an unwavering faith in divine justice, the notion that those who suffer on Earth will have a better life in the hereafter. By nature, we are pessoptimists—if half of our land is burned down, we thank the heavens for the remaining half. We revere life, and all the things that make life possible, and if we venerate bread, it's only because we embrace life from the depths of our being. We say Yes to life, even when the rest of the world seems to say otherwise. We say No to death, a resounding No that can be heard from a long distance away, if you care to listen. Yes, we tend to take our pain lightly; yes, we are schooled in the ways of suffering, but we still give death the sanctity it deserves, for we are humans, all too human, and we will lament and pine over our dead like all people do.

Someone has died. I can tell from the eerie silence into which he's slowly drifted. He's been gasping his dying breaths for hours, screaming out feebly. Then the screams faded into a constant whimper, the music stopped, and we heard him no more. Perhaps he's sleeping, dreaming up his fantastical meal, for his mouth is still agape and showing signs of extreme hunger. He was an old man, with a long white beard and a frail body, thinner than a tree branch—so incredibly thin it could fit in a tree hollow, which is not just a metaphor, as we have run out of coffins and the graveyards filled up. No one is trying to wake him up; perhaps he has no one, no surviving soul to grieve for him or lament his absence. He barely has himself left, having dwindled into mere bones in which hardly a trace of his former self has been retained. It's a sad way to go, though in our state of prolonged torture, the cold hand of death can hardly strike sooner.

I have heard people wishing for death, pleading for it. If you wonder why they never attempt to hasten it themselves, by taking their own lives, or embarking on a mass suicide, or perhaps choosing a more merciful way to go, it's not merely because their spiritual dignity forbids it, but because they have no energy left in them to commit it. Look at me, I barely have enough strength in my body to kill a bird, which I would do gladly, except that the poor creatures have perished from hunger, for this is right now a place where a piece of grain is more treasured than gold. I can hardly hold a knife in my frail condition, let alone send it home. I smile at the memory of my mother. I remember when I was a boy, in the first flush of manhood, and she summoned me to slaughter a pigeon for her, and I passed out before the bird was dead. She cooked stuffed baby birds for lunch—that rococo homeland delicacy never ceased to delight! It was so satisfying we licked our fingers with joy. We ate, and asked for more, and she would fetch us more and say, in her whimsical way, that if we kept at it, we could ultimately grow wings and fly. That woman was devoted to my belly, as if my survival was her cross to bear. She always pleaded with me to eat. She stuffed morsels of food in my mouth, and when food became scarce, which was often, fed me morality tales on the virtues of contentment and forbearance.

The Good Lord and the woman who gives away half a pomegranate, her only possession, to the poor. The good king and the poor woman who stirs stones into her soup pot to coax her starving children to sleep. This morning, I recalled this last tale with a sad grin when I met a woman who sat by her tent stirring water in a large pot, which contained nothing but stones, and feigned fish soup. Her starved little children shifted around her with their rawboned bodies and empty bellies, staring at the pot through their hollow eyes, stirring in their agitated state like sleepless devils. I smile at the memory of my mother, who mastered the art of deception to perfection, though ultimately, the trick would lose its ability and the magic turned at last on the magician when my hapless mother died of hunger.

Life was a tolerable hell. It was not a paradise, but we endured it. We ate on the floor because of the relentless bombing. When the house shook, and furniture wobbled, we sat on the ground and ate our food in haste. We ate in fear, and we feared nothing like dying with a morsel still in our mouth, or a meal left uneaten. Our parents told stories of the exiled ancestors who took their dough in haste, clotheslines still hanging, food left uneaten, water boiling, coffee brewing. Oh, the morning coffee! I hardly remember the last time I savored it, enjoyed its fatal aroma mingled with smokes of war. My father died craving it, yearning for a last glimpse of it. Our people live for coffee. That's why we never sleep. Drinking coffee creates the illusion of a new day, a new beginning. Our ancestors believed coffee was a sacred beverage from heaven imbued with earthly love. It's an emblem of generosity. We luxuriate in coffeemaking, and when coffee becomes scarce, which is often, we too still stir little stones in boiling water for the sheer pretense of it—as you can plainly tell from the sight of these old men. They have gathered around a small fire and taken to stirring their water in earnest, as if savoring their own delusion. Nothing more exotic can be imagined under this siege than a real pot of coffee! It can take us days to brew one. We sit by the fire indulging in leisurely talk, smoking our pipes, weaving our tales, weighing with slow relish the chances of war and prospects of peace. Sadly, this raging hunger is now threatening to render our lives mere dust, like the dark residue of coffee.

The breadline has swollen into a massive gathering of starving people, a nation on the brink of mass starvation. No, not on the brink, for the people *are* starving, have been for days, and it's a miracle they have survived thus far. I wade through this great gathering of the hungry, flooding steadily toward the gates as if jockeying for the secret gate to heaven. Except there is no heaven behind this hell. Who knew hell was crowded with the oppressed! There is hardly space to put your empty bowl. Sometimes, when the day rumbles on and the keen sun beams down, people would place the empty pots on their heads for shade. Or when it rains, which is quite rare, they would raise the pots to the sky and fill them up with rainwater, and hydrate their parched throats—though oftentimes, thanks to the relentless bombing, the rain comes down ashen and mingled with the smoke of war, sparking lively debates over whether water fills you up or rather kindles your craving for food. People here never tire of telling the old joke about a poor father who notices that his insatiable son eats too much, and he slaps him squarely in the face, saying: "Drink more, and eat less, for water shall fill you up!" And when the son retorts that water only enhances his appetite for food, the father, realizing his mistake, slaps the boy harder still for failing to warn him earlier. No, it was not my father; I would've remembered if a hot red slap whizzed over my face! My father was of the kinder breed, the kind of father who suffered hunger in silence while his children binged on—until one day he too gave up the fight and lucked out without so much as a last meal.

Being an orphan is hardly special in this war-torn hell. But you long for your parents, yes, especially at night, when hunger overtakes you and you burst out weeping.

Time heals, but it does not make you forget. Sometimes my late father visits me in my dreams, but he never stays the night. Mother would visit if she could, but her knees are acting up. Even in heaven, we are haunted by pain. For the fact is that if you search a camp on foot for days on end, foraging for food like a bewildered wolf to save your starving children, ultimately, your knees act up. My father was a strong man in his better days. He had strong hands, a proud chin, a broad chest, fearless eyes, and a good heart to boot. He was a bravehearted man, a good Samaritan, a stalwart farmer who never broke. He was a gentleman, when men here could still be gentle. But this is no country for strong men or noble souls. It's a jungle, where only the vicious survive. I promised him I would survive, and I shall cling to life until death tears us apart. I shall survive, yes, if only to defy death and avenge my father, my poor humble people who never knew peace on this Earth, the men and women who perished in the dark, who lived and died claiming their place in the sun.

The sun had set not long ago, and the moon had sailed into the desolate sky like a loaf of homemade bread, promising another night of absolute deprivation.

People have scrambled toward the gates, which remain sealed. There is no escaping the siege. It's like a vast panopticon, swollen with the hungry and displaced, and trampled by two million feet. We are besieged by land, air, and sea. There is nowhere safe to flee. The one time I ventured beyond the border walls was on foot. It was quite memorable, for I met death on the road. Memory blurs as to which direction I walked in. I remember wandering for hours, descending from the mountain to the sea, meandering from land to desert, traversing hostile terrain with no end in sight, landmines, buried in the last war, lying under the road. I could feel the mines ticking beneath my feet, chilling the very marrow of my bones. There was nothing alive or stirring save for a batch of unsmiling soldiers perched in their watchtowers, hollering out in hostile staccato, and waving me backward, forward, sideways—back to the prison. Nowhere was safe, and the land was just as formidable as the sky. In hindsight, it was a tad delusional of me to imagine that flight was within reach. It was laughable to think that I could coax reality into my little fantasy of escape.

There was no breaking the siege, and I knew it. The siege is our destiny, and there is no denying one's destiny. As our wisemen say, there's no hope of breaking out this prison without crushing the gates on ourselves. It would take a miracle to break free, like being abducted by space aliens and beamed out of this doomed place, or perhaps saved by your ancestorial spirits and resurrected in heaven. The best we could do is seal our grievances in a bottle and cast them into the open sea. Resistance? Excuse me if I laugh, but wherever did people resist on empty stomachs? We can barely stand on our feet without falling flat into the abyss. Resistance is like fire; you need to feed it constantly to keep it ablaze. Hunger is the only fire that feeds on itself.

All my life, I have dreamed of escape. It started as a fantasy. It was wartime—always wartime—and I watched the stars waiting for a sign, an omen, a herald, a flying carpet, a spaceship, to beam me away. Far off in the distance, I spotted a dim light like a distant star. It was red-blue, made of sun and sky, and my feet burned to set out for it. It shone where the sky touched the sea on the horizon. Beyond the horizon was darkness, and beyond the darkness the free world. I can still see that dim red light. It flashes suddenly through the gloom, and just as sudden, fades away. Perhaps it's the blood in my eyes. Or maybe there was no light. Perhaps the whole thing was a mirage, the residue of a bad dream, for I was a hell of a dreamer. I can't be sure. Only death is certain. You can't trust your eyes in this hellscape, where nothing but dust breathes. When you're a child, you allowed yourself to dream, to fancy yourself flying on a mythical bird, or riding a horse, or a donkey. But it's ludicrous at my age to indulge in these fantasies, for you must accept your doom and face reality with courage, in its full scope, and dreamless cruelty. You must see the world without filters—a sprawling wilderness where only wolves survive.

I wonder if the outside world remembers us. Or knows about our existence. Or at least understands that, like all people, we have dreams and hopes. We are not as naïve as we sound. We have hope for the future because it's all we have left. We are futuristic by nature; it's how we endure interminable indignity. We see the world from the prism of the stars, the moon and the sun, the chances of rain, the prospects of harvest, and the heralds of spring. I remember my grandmother poring over my palm or reading the stars to divine my future, not knowing that when the sky falls down, the stars fall silent. We scan the sky and read omens in the stars; if the heavens comply with our predictions, we say we are following our stars. Or we die waiting; then no harm is done. We fold up our prayer mats, embrace our lot, and toil on. Otherwise, we dig tunnels and scurry underground, and like all people, go under when the earth trembles and things fall apart, and emerge when the sky rises. Then we bury our dead without ceremony and go about our lives.

But we are not cavemen; we tunnel down so often only because our besiegers are denying us our place under the sun. Show us the light and we will perform miracles; and this land abounds with earthly miracles, from the river to the sea, and for all the destruction, it still retains a vestige of its lost beauty and former glory. This land you see was a beautiful mother once, the envy of all. She was a sun-kissed paradise where God and all his otherworldly promises had no purchase. It was peaceful, prelapsarian, a promised land. It was a pleasure just to behold the beauty of the sunset upon the sea. Then war came, and all that disappeared. Humans invaded, fire burgeoned, and natives fell. Those who survived scattered and dispersed. Those who remained were allowed to die in silence.

But it isn't all gloom, for we can hear the promised tucks growling beyond the walls, charging our way, timidly but firmly. Children hold their empty bowls overhead, gazing through their hollowed eyes, poking their tiny heads and shoving their pleading hands with force through the narrow gaps in the fences, where nothing seems to fill up the bowls but the waiting void. They subsist on wonderfully little hope, and the bellows of the flour trucks marching in the distance—the sound of our salvation. Hope is a strange thing; it keeps you alive, even when it seems to die with each passing hour. But what do we have but hope, broken promises, broken hearts, and broken lives?

And we wait, and wait, and what do we have but waiting? Refuge is the art of waiting. For many years, we have sat in our impoverished camps and waited for something to happen. Yet nothing ever happens, nothing but wars, and more wars, and still other wars. Every war brings more misery and displacement. Look at me, I have been displaced so often that I have stopped counting. War after war, I have become accustomed to displacement. I have *cemented* my displacement. I have no home and no location. Dislocation *is* my location. Twenty years a refugee, born and raised in captivity, and I have endured it. I have taken my toll lightly and bravely.

Endless wars have made us hardy people. We seem to have acquired, in our state of constant deprivation, certain survival instincts, a rare kind of steadfastness that seems to baffle outsiders. We never beg or grovel. We suffer in silence, but we never break. We endure and carry on. We make do and pull together. We persist and hold out. Exile us, and we pitch our tents and praise God for the fresh air. We thank heaven and carry on with our miserable lives. Bomb our homes, and we will find a hole in the ruins to fill with water and bathe our children. Blow up our houses, and we will find a toehold amid the rubble to sit and fill our pipes, and smoke the pain away. Destroy our land, and a new homeland, hills, olive groves, and orange trees, will bloom in the hearts of our children. What does not kill us makes us more steadfast.

It's hunger that's killing us, devouring us one after another. I always fasted as a child. I fasted to please God and my father. The trick is to go hungry enough to hallucinate that you are in heaven, where everything comes to you by merely wishing it. One day, I fancied that God was my chef. It was a delicious dream, while it lasted. God rewarded those who fasted. Or so I was told. But this hunger has no reward. It's a slow, agonizing death, and it's torturous while it lasts. Give me a piece of bread dipped in homegrown olive oil, and I will die a happy man! I'm not afraid of death, but people ought to die with dignity. Even imprisoned killers awaiting death are offered a last meal. I have never killed anyone. I'm the one being killed, slowly but surely. Every hour promises to be the last. Give me my last supper and let me die a martyr, for I have reached the last threshold of my endurance. Give me bread, plain, ungarnished bread—all the same. Prolonged hunger and the daily exposure to death have dulled our taste buds.

War has blunted our sense of smell. In fact, I barely had one. For years, I lived without it, which was a blessing in disguise. When I was born, I inhaled a strange chemical unleashed by a bomb, and lost my sense of smell. There was nothing I could smell—not perfume, nor flowers, nor my mother's delicious cooking, which was a torture, for I could see the aroma of her homemade food wafting in the air and filling the house like magic mist. And so, I accepted my doom, until one day my father brought me a cube of olive oil soap, which was of the brown quality and resembled a chocolate bar. And I could smell it, yes, I could smell the powerful, fruity aroma of the green olives of the homeland. "I can smell! I can smell!" I cried out, whereupon my father, tears streaming down his face, stormed into the shower and embraced me.

Give me bread, plain bread, made of flour, water, and salt. We can do without the yeast. For the water is Godsent, the salt is given by the sea, but the flour—if you spoke our mother tongue, you would be startled to discover that in our language bread also translates as *life*, which to us is more than mere etymological coincidence. For bread *is* life, and no one can take it away from us without imposing a death sentence on those who venerate it. So, if you visit our war-torn quarters and chance upon a starving child screaming from the top of his lungs, "Give me life! Give me life!" he's probably asking for bread.

I shove my way through a sea of starving masses, feeling feeble and exhausted, while still battling, with whatever vigor left in me, the roaring fires within—wondering, in my battered mind, whether this flour rumor is true, or just another oasis invented in the zeal of our parched and delirious imagination. Flour, that magic elixir of life, how do I yearn for a last glimpse of you! How do I crave the strength to stand unshaken and scream out, Give me life! Give me life!

And beyond the flour seekers, the breadline has swelled into a great multitude of displaced people holding bundles and carring their homes on their backs like snails. They are clearly homeless, dispossessed, without so much as a tent. They sleep on the bare earth and stretch their arms under their heads for pillows. They appear to be hopeful refugees, following rumors of possible exile. Now and then, our besiegers open an escape route, a one-way passage, with no return. Most people decide to stay put and die on their soil. Others take the route to permanent displacement. It's a great gathering of exiles. People of all stripes marching on foot. Men and women, with dusty faces and dirty clothes, headed for the unknown. Children bundled up, loaded on donkey carts and wheelbarrows, bound for the unknown.

I cast my gaze over this ebbing sea of humanity. There is an old woman, aged ninety, perhaps older, waiting with a bundle that seems to weigh her down. She appears to struggle on foot. Leaning on her cane, treading lightly, she winds her way through the crowd, not too slow, but not too fast; she seems in no hurry to be exiled. Her baffled eyes gaze briefly through the waiting crowd, as if seeking someone, and it's in that perplexed gaze that I conclude that she's likely blind.

She is older than the camp itself. Her aspects are geological, her face ancient, her eyes deep and hollowed. The wrinkles on her face resemble the barks of an old olive tree. Everything about her is old and ancient, except her eyes, which are brown, like the soil that hatched her. There is a sense of irrevocable loss in her eyes that no words can contain. I look into her eyes and see a woman who has lost everything. A woman who suffered grave injustices in the past, and who suffers still. I see my grandmother, the good old refugee who suffers in silence, but stands fast and never breaks, like a deep-rooted tree. I see a woman made in the image of her motherland: fragile on the outside, stout and resilient within. A woman who, despite all the suffering, still refuses to accept her doom, clinging to her right to live and survive. On her face, I see the history of all the injustices inficted on this place. In her eyes, I see a woman who has lived and outlived the grand annals of wars and starvation. A woman who has spent her golden years under siege, with no way in or out. Years of oppression have brought her no justice and no relief, nothing but constant indignity. A woman who has been betrayed by the world. A woman who has been denied the right to die in dignity. A woman who has been robbed of her humanity. A woman who has lost faith in humankind. She may not survive this war, and it's doubtful she will complete the journey on foot, but her face will haunt me for years to come, should I survive that long.

By the time I awake from my sad reverie, the old woman has faded into the crowd, vanishing like a phantom in this sea of the displaced.

There is something about hunger that makes you forget about the grand demands of war and peace: freedom, justice, and other lofty abstractions. We have been under siege for so long that we hardly remember what freedom is like. They say the road to freedom is long and red with martyrdom. Our besiegers would rather have us starve and revert to cannibalism, just to prove to the world that we are less than human, not knowing that we would rather die of starvation than eat our own flesh. For even as we gather here pleading for flour, we are still highly dignified people. We revel in the art of sacrifice, and our sacrifices verge on martyrdom. When war hits, and food becomes scarce, our fathers would sit in silence, battle the fires of hunger bravely, and watch us eat our food like ravening cubs. They would be lucky to find a decent morsel of fish left to eat, or a handful of crumbs of stale bread to dip in their soup, or a mouthful of bone marrow to suck out. Having survived the unsung martyrdom, they would crack the bones and suck the marrow dry and slurp the uneaten residue of the soup pot in which they were cooked. My father was like that. He was a martyr for his children. He was not the kind of father who would sacrifice his son at the altar to please his God. If he had to sacrifice, he would gladly offer himself. Which he ultimately did. How do you suppose I was orphaned at an early age and learned to fend for myself in this human jungle where the weak perish and only the predators survive?

But you won't hear me weep, because I'm a dignified young man, and the seed of dignified people who, for all the torment and humiliation, refuse to bow down. We are hopeful by nature. Throw a siege on us, starve us, bomb us, displace us, deny us our place under the sun, and we will still cling to our land like the indestructible roots of our olive trees. There's no way of uprooting us without killing us, which only reunites us with the soil. We would drench the soil with our blood if it comes to that, and it's not just an idle metaphor, for there come times when the land becomes so soaked in red it resembles the surface of Mars. But we are not barbarians or ghouls, though the sweat we gather on the road makes us look bad. We smell of dried blood only because we've fled our bombed homes before we had a chance to bathe. Still, we hold on to our dignity. We endure and stand fast. We carry on and resist, yes, if only to assert our humanity. Sometimes, when our pain becomes too much to endure, we throw our hands up in desperation, give up the struggle, and embrace our lot. But we won't eat our own flesh. We would starve sooner than eat our own flesh. We would die a thousand deaths before we descend into barbarism. And we have proven it. The streets are teeming with them, men and women who have perished of starvation, and who would rather let themselves be eaten by stray animals than be the animals.

You see a wild dog, clasping the body of a dead child between its sharp blood-soaked teeth, roaming the streets in a rushed search for a quiet cozy corner to sit down and enjoy its lunch, seeming visibly weakened by hunger, yet still a dog at heart, with enough strength remaining in its bones to tear at the dead and wreak havoc on the living. Sadly, we had no time to save the poor soul; we hardly had the strength to tear him from the hound's teeth. The child could have feasted on the weak hound when he had the chance, but he accepted his doom, lucked out, and died bravely. Because he was a dignified little one, the seed of a dignified people.

But we are humans, and like everyone on this Earth, we need food to survive. No people can subsist on dignity alone. Dignity be damned! It has brought us nothing but pain and suffering. What has it availed us, this pride? They say it's for freedom's sake, justice's sake—excuse me if I laugh again, but no one can survive on lofty promises of freedom and justice. No one can subsist on rosy images of divine justice and eternal happiness. We want happiness and justice *now*, on this Earth, while we are alive and have the power to savor it!

Give me a hot piece of bread dipped in the green emeralds of our olive oil! We can live by bread alone. For we are rough people, and we rough it until better days come. We can endure the same meal every day, and eat whatever the earth yields and produces of herbs, and cucumbers, and garlic, and lentils, and radishes, and beets, and onions. When hunger hits, we hold our noses and eat whatever the worms have left out. It's not like we are asking for eggs, or rice, or meat, or other forbidden luxuries. Or chocolate, which is strictly banned here, for it fills our men with bad energy, or so our oppressors believe. God forbid we should ever crave chocolate! How can we crave something we've never tasted? They say it's dark but sweet. We hear it grows on trees somewhere. My father too believed that chocolate was a luxury. Or perhaps he simply could not afford it. Was he in league with the oppressors? He said dates were sweeter, so whenever I longed for chocolate, I dug into dates. When those became scarce, I would suck on sugar canes, which abounded here once.

We hear of places where children eat chocolate eggs for dessert! I hardly remember what a real egg looks like, except that it's oval and made of white flesh. My first sin was stealing an egg from a neighbor's farm, which you could hardly call a sin, for I was hungry then, and eggs abounded in plenty in these quarters. Now, a child finds a raw egg for the first time in months; he holds it with trembling hands lest it break, like a surgeon holding a human heart. Clinging fast to it with both hands, he does not bother to wipe his happy tears, for he knows the egg can be a lifesaver, even when there's little left to live for. A raw egg, nothing more exotic can be imagined in this nonplace! No, we are not asking for edible flowers to garnish our food—*flour* is what we are asking for. The rest is luxury. We have no appetite for luxury, comfort food, or fine dining. We demand bread because we believe it's God-given, and we pray to God to give us this day our daily bread. We believe in the covenant of bread, that no human being should be denied it. You have no right to starve us. Nobody has, not even our daily bread giver who dwells in heaven.

We are minimalists, from want and destitution, not out of some urban luxury. We hear of places where people die not of hunger, but from gluttony, overeating, dying a most luxurious death, full and sated, perhaps too full and sated. Good for them. No happier death can be imagined. Between dying hungry and dying from gluttony, I would choose gluttony every time. Imagine my agony, envying dead people! But as people say here, Death is the surest meal.

But remember, there's a special circle in hell for gluttony. Overeating is a sin here. We have a special punishment for those who overeat while others starve. It's crude and mannerless. Even camels, to debunk the legend, do not overeat; they merely store fat in their humps as an energy reserve, which they deploy when food becomes scarce. I was a victim of that legend myself, and there was a time, a long time ago, when I let myself be completely fooled by its fabled allure. I was a child then, and like all children, I was terrified by the prospect of prolonged hunger. Whenever war raged and starvation loomed, I gorged like a camel in peacetime and made myself sick and more likely to die from gluttony than starvation. I would nauseate and vomit, vowing never to eat again—a vow I would break so often it was rendered meaningless, like the day I went on a sugar binge and locked myself in a room, chowed down on homemade sweets until I was too fat to exit from the door, and so sick I never touched sugar again. I despised myself for it and would continue to abhor it till the next war raged on. The sheer memory of those days makes me sick to my stomach. My only regret, now I'm starving and nearly dead, is not binging enough to put myself off food permanently.

In our state of sad martyrdom, we feel like that hunger artist who starves himself to death in his vainglorious pursuit of fame, except that people here have not chosen to starve; they are being starved by a force that tolerates no martyrdom and can never be made to understand it. Hunger is like an invisible weapon to them, and they deploy it with mad passion and without an inkling of the torture it inflicts on us. Or perhaps they have a penchant for sadism. A bomb kills you in seconds, but hunger kills you in weeks—days and nights of a drawn-out, agonizing death that renders bombing a sweet prospect.

I have learned that the worst wounds are the ones that are invisible. Hunger is a colorless torture that bleeds constantly inside you. It preys on your blood like some camouflaged leech, and sponges off you like a bloodsucker. The monster is invisible, yes, but the ravage it wreaks on people is too palpable to unsee. Look at me, I can hardly recognize myself. I seem a stranger to myself, an alien, a ghoul. I'm someone else, robbed of my features, a shell of my former self, a dying mortal sliding nearer and nearer to the abyss. I can hear the echo of my bones clattering together on the ravaged grounds with a dry, hard rattle.

I have lost my bearings. I feel weak and feeble, delirious with pain and exhaustion. But it isn't all gloom, for I can hear the clamor of trucks approaching, like happy visions sailing into the vacant spaces of my starved imagination. One feels like walking before a fallen Tower of Babel. Except people here have nowhere to disperse, for they are locked under siege, sealed in behind high walls and gates, stranded between desert and sea. As I wade through a sea of starving masses, one thought terrifies me still. What if, in the mad rush for flour, we stampede to death? What if a flour war breaks out? It would be a war within a war, from which no survivor will emerge save for the wolves, and all the sheep will likely trample underfoot and die a death of unspeakable agony. I fear for the little children, and the beaten men and women who have no fight left in them. It terrifies me to think that this promised flour, the token of our salvation, could become our burial dust, our white coffins. What if the flour proves poisoned? What if those flour bags turn out to be the last nails hammered to our cross? It's not unprecedented in these quarters. Haven't our besiegers poisoned our water wells and grain mills to starve us?

Many have died in the bombing, which is as relentless and inescapable as the air we breathe. Even the rain takes a breath! There are many untold cruelties in this world, nothing crueler than bombing people on the brink of starvation, killing them amid their dreamless deprivation. Have you ever seen a child, lying lifeless on the roadside, a morsel of food still hanging in his gaping mouth? I have, and it's not a pretty sight. A child deprived of his last meal—no death more impatient can be imagined. People say the kid was trying to hasten his meal when the bomb swooped down and snatched it out of his throat like a vulture tearing at its prey. This explains people's rush to hurry their last meal, for there is no shortage of children who, in the mad hope of cheating death, shovel food in their mouths as if served consecrated bread or a last sacrament. Sadly, there's no food left to hurry, and in the frantic race between food and death, the latter seems to outpace the former. Surely, you've heard of the young men who found a pair of eggs and dashed to make a traditional dish of eggs and tomatoes. As they stood there admiring the slowly cooked eggs nestling in the tomato sauce, olive oil bubbling in the hot skillet, a bomb cut short their gastronomic yearning.

As I hang there brooding over these sad tales of food and death, a bewildered boy breaks into hysterical tears when he seizes upon a make-believe charity meal for the first time in days; they are not tears of happiness, but tears of confusion and disbelief, and the fear of losing his Godsent meal. Not waiting to reach his tent, he thrashes about as if he is devouring the meal entirely, staggering through the crowd like a famished motherless cub flanked by packs of hungry lions. How many moments of happiness that meal will buy him is hard to tell, but the joy of beating death has clearly overtaken his imagination.

A splitting headache takes hold of me, a constant throb that refuses to go away. My head is lighter than a feather, and my body too frail to hold me, but my heart is heavy, as if shoring up some invisible cross. My growling belly is a frightful emptiness filled with raging flames. Hunger is a torment like no other. It renders you a phantom, a ghost of your former self, a spirit hovering over the desolate landscape with no clear idea why he's still alive. But you are not deluded, for you know that you live on borrowed time, in a borrowed place, with a borrowed heart and borrowed eyes to weep for yourself, and that you are alive only because the angel of death is busy reaping other lives nearby.

Surviving hunger is death postponed. For even if you survive hunger, there are a hundred other ways to die in this hellscape. They say that if you survive the bombing, and evade the rubble, and escape the flying shrapnel, and dodge the sniper's bullets, and outrun the fires, and endure the cold, and outlive the diseases, and outlast the plague, and a thousand other maladies we never knew existed, then you may have a chance to live. Perhaps there is some mercy in dying in the first instant of bombing, vanishing instantly, in your sleep, amid your dreams, without so much as a scream—and being spared the horrors that followed.

And besides the raging fires, there is the torture of agonizing screams. For even if you endure hunger, there is no escaping the howls of children crying constantly in your ears, because nothing you could do would assuage the fires inside them. A thousand clowns would fail to soothe their agony. The ancestral trick of stirring rocks in a pot to lull them to sleep has lost its allure. The helpless poor souls have boundless energy and little endurance, and must be fed this minute, without tricks or suspension. Lying will only inflame their craving and prolong the torture. And they could always tell, if not from your hopeless tone and giveaway features, then from your restless and excessive fidgeting. They know you're not cooking them food, but merely cooking up hope where nothing gleams but the dark glint of despair. I was a child once, you know.

There is a child, an obviously hungry child. For hours, he's been sucking his toe, and weeping, sucking and weeping. Sometimes, he dazes briefly into painful delirium, but soon resumes the ritual, with renewed eagerness. Besides him a little boy sits picking his nose and licking his finger, licking and picking, while weeping through the process. Then he would lick his tears, and finding them salty, satiate himself with water, which fills him briefly, before he resumes the ritual.

I hang there watching the children with bemused curiosity, not knowing whether to laugh or weep. My throat parched as a desert, my eyes riddled with dust and too dry to weep, I content myself with a yellow, sickly smile.

I feast on memories of better times. My mother cooked fine food. It was delicious, earthy, and gratifying. I regret not eating it all. "What's cooking, Mom?" My favorite words! She cooked with fire, in old ancestral pots, and not without imagination. Even the bread was a delight, and there came days when we lived by bread alone. For dessert, we had carob pudding, of course, which was heaven in a bowl and worked magic on the children. We ate it, and then watched every cell in our body shake with ravenous gratitude. Life was simple. We did not live in the lap of luxury, but we wanted for nothing. We roughed it. When war hit, people survived on whatever the wild earth yielded. When it's your land, you accept whatever destiny offers you. In the last war, people survived on grains they fetched from animal manure, which they called *caviar*. With any luck, they would fetch out a bean or a corn kernel. Many were reduced to eating grass and leafy greens, which turned their faces so green they resembled little aliens. Many of us have survived that way. Others would resort to eating insects, provided they existed. Or rotten food, which tasted like blue cheese, but better. You hold your nose, nuke it with salt, and wash it down with water. When hunger hits, you discover a new species in yourself. Wartime food is not for the fainthearted. It's marginally preferable to hunger. If you see a child making the expression of someone who's swallowed a bad oyster, you can tell he's been fed wartime junk. You can never tell the food from its taste or smell;

the bread has no smell and tastes like a sponge. The fruits have no flavor, and the meat is untraceable to its source animal. But you eat what comes, and feed your heart on reveries of better times. If a child finds an apple with a worm inside; he simply closes his eyes, holds his nose, and devours it. Hunger is the best sauce, as they say.

The sad tragedy is that these wartime substances are a luxury now and scarcely exist outside the realm of memory. One is lucky to find a handful of grain, or a parcel of grass, or a rotten fruit, or anything formerly food. Even the caviars have vanished, the little grains that once sustained our ancestors. But hope keeps us alive, even when that hope appears to be nothing but a mirage, a glad rumor invented in our sad hallucinations. What if the flour rumor proves nothing but a floral fantasy, a figment of our starved imagination? We could die waiting, perish in our dreamless hallucinations. It's not far-fetched, for even as we stand in the line waiting, holding our empty pots and waiting, we can see people drop with frightful thuds, dead or alive, it's hard to tell. Like dominoes they fall; some briefly come to, but others never rise again.

To help the children cope, parents have invented pretend food, a blend of sand, clay, rubble, and leaves. Or plastic toys resembling food, which are more torturing than soothing. And you know the whole place has gone berserk when vendors start selling pretend food, and people buy into the delicious illusion and play along, and before long, the streets fill up with imaginary feasts, and fanciful banquets, and the inevitable cacophony and clatter of utensils and food preparation! Sometimes, catering to the madness, I picture a grand feast, an open buffet, with an infinite assortment of bread and meat. I fancy a street full of tables set for a grand banquet, illuminated by holiday candle lights and lanterns, and flanked by giant cauldrons full of golden soup, aromatic smoke flying out of them and filling the air, bubbles surfacing them with enchanted majesty. Coffee boiling, teapots whistling, milk foaming, bread baking.

Inadvertently, my shattered mind drifts to visions of cannibalism, which I resist and banish from my mind with the last shred of mental power left in me, like Adam fighting the temptation of a forbidden fruit. I'm starting to suspect that Eve ate the forbidden fruit because she was hungry, and that she would've gobbled up Adam if she had a good knife or knew how to kill. It would take a cosmic fall to Earth for humans to learn these skills, which they would master as soon as they landed. Humans are wired to kill. Or so the sacred books teach us. But they are not meant to eat their own flesh. They are more like wild cats that kill for fun but seldom feed on their prey. And yet the thoughts keep thronging and bouncing back, and I keep resisting, exerting greater mental effort every time, which only exacerbates my pain and exhausts my soul.

Soon, I find myself roaming in an existential haze, wandering a mental desert without oasis, too hungry to sleep and too tired to stay awake. Perhaps this truck convoy is nothing but a mirage, a decoy to raise our hopes, then crush them mercilessly, to the bemusement of our besiegers. It's not unprecedented in these quarters to mock people to death by means of false hopes.

Time passes slowly in this inferno. I have lost my sense of it. And of space, too. I live mainly in the dark, empty spaces of my deprivation. I pass the time weaving out images of food and subsisting on memories of old swallows that once delighted my heart. Homemade bread, with a spread of fresh olive oil and sugar. Olive oil, wine of the poor, which abounded in those autumns of our content. Homegrown oranges, sour in the mouth, sweet in the heart. Lentil, meat of the deprived! We guzzled it so often our faces waxed yellow, like the flesh of a lemon. And to think that we resisted it! "It's full of iron," my mother would plead in exasperation. She always pleaded with me to eat. "For heaven's sake, son, you look like a cinnamon stick!" Skinny, she called me. Or Bony, when my body dwindled enough to warrant the name. My father's ultimate pleasure was watching us eat while quietly saluting himself for it. He would stand there and watch us with satisfied admiration, crying out: "Dig in! Dig in!" He was not the kind of father who would let his children go hungry. I remember when I was five and fasted to please God; I started out gravely, before I began to shrivel toward sunset and nearly fainted, whereupon my father, feeling sorry for his brave little lamb, rushed toward me with a glass of water and a handful of dates. "Eat this!" he said. "Don't be a martyr!" Hunger was no game, and my kindhearted father knew it.

Life was not a paradise, but it was tolerable. I remember with a faint smile my school days in the camp. One day, our art teacher asked us to draw an apple, and we sat there staring at him through our dumbfounded eyes, for we had never seen an apple before, and had no inkling of how to draw one. Then he asked us to draw a camp under siege, and the image simply jumped out of our pencils and filled the blank pages in vivid and horrifying detail. Our tree of knowledge consisted of high walls and sealed gates and mined borders; there was hardly a fruit on it.

Oh, the apple, noblest of all fruits! Give me an apple, and let me sin and fall! It would be delicious to munch on one, suck out its juice, and put out the fires within. "Apple of my eye," my mother cuddled me. Or maybe an orange, a bloody orange for my bone-dry blood! Or perhaps grapes, sweet, sour treats to soothe down our wrath! Or sunbeaten pomegranates, the color of blood! Or a handful of sweet homemade cookies made of the soft, tender flour of the homeland, and stuffed with dates. Or those golden sunlike holiday cookies, filled with walnuts, baked with love, buttered and glazed to perfection, adorned with sesame seeds, powdered with soft sugar—would that be too much to ask of fate?

My delicious reverie is cut short by the blaring approach of aid trucks, which rings loud and true because more people can testify to it. This rumble is louder than the sea, and its promise higher than all the heavens that betrayed us and fell silent as we starved! God is testing our resolve, the faithful among us would say, though if God really meant to intervene in our misery, he would have done so by now. A truck is drawing near. I can hear its mighty roar, like the sound of a thousand waves. No, I'm not hallucinating, for I can see a rainbow in the clouds, a sign of hope and joy. It appears to me that the heavens and earth had passed away, and a new paradise was rolled together here. Who knew that paradise was compressed in a bowl of flour! But happiness is personal. You see a child, dashing away with a pair of torn shoes he's found in the rubble, sheer happiness writ large on his face, and you realize that all those global indexes of happiness are but a utopian fallacy. Can you tell me for certain that people who eat three meals a day are three times happier than those who eat almost nothing?

On they vroom, creating a symphony of wailing engines. Cheers erupt. Children dance, women ululate, and men, hapless creatures of God who have seen their children die slowly before their eyes, weep from relief and nearly collapse in tears. Even the little birds are back chirping. The place resembles a resurrection site. The empty bowls will soon fill up, and people will bake their bread in haste, and eat it before they lose the strength to start a fire and knead the dough, and make the bread of life, and tell the little ones that whoever comes to me shall not starve or go hungry. We have already set up the stone ovens, summoned the bakers, and fetched the firewood, which we saved from our burned trees.

There is no denying that the flour trucks are headed our way. The approaching din, the clatter and rattle on the road, is now the sound of life about to be reborn, for there is no way to describe the people here but as walking dead. Look at the poor children. They smell of dust and dry blood. They look tired and worn out, visibly exhausted, with diminished bodies and frail features, yellow teeth, bare feet, and open wounds still bleeding. And yet they look happy, or perhaps sadly resilient, like little fawns bleating in silence. A girl stands there smiling through her surviving eye, grateful she still has one. You see a boy standing on one leg, or holding his bowl with his good hand, with a hopeful smile visible on his face that shames hope itself. You see fearfully thin children, with sunburned faces and dusty eyes, standing barefoot in the line, waiting with excited anticipation, smiling their toothless smiles. One child stands wearing olive battle fatigues and combat boots that seem to suck him in. It brings to mind the soldier's boots my father bought me once, for braving the mud, enduring winter, marching over hostile terrain, playing soldiers and rebels. They were meant to instill fear in my foes. Or so I believed. Sadly, our romance was short-lived. One night there was a curfew and I was on my way home, chanting, marching in a soldierly fashion, when a military jeep lurched past and suddenly pulled over in a great cloud of dust, while faceless soldiers jumped off, seized me, stripped me naked, hung my boots from my ears and left me in the middle of the street, shivering in the darkness, weeping and trembling in their wake. It was an act of senseless violence that left me more bewildered than wounded. What happened that night is still a puzzle to me. When the jeep stopped, and the other boys darted away in fear, for some mysterious reason that still eludes me, I stood my ground, rooted to the spot as if struck by lightning. Was I too afraid to run away? Or was I perhaps overcome by my misplaced bravado, overtaken by my deluded sense of fellowship with the soldiers, believing my combat boots would somehow protect me? Innocent times.

I labor to keep myself from falling as I slowly trudge through this gathering of the hungry, and imagine my inexplicable fright when I glimpse my battered face in a waiting pot, reflected to me in the most deplorable state a human face can find itself. I never did imagine, not even in my worst nightmares, and I have had my fill of those, that one day I would be afraid of myself. I'm visibly tired and depleted, the dried blood from the first bombing still caked on me. My face is blanched with horror. My heart is aching, my eyes two balls of dust, my head burning hot, throbbing like a ticking bomb. My body is petering out to a thin skin. I haven't eaten for days. I feel weaker than a spider's net. I look frail and noticeably diminished. I'm cold and sick besides, sweating like a naked seal. My body hasn't seen water for weeks. My clothes are dirty, blood-stained, clinging to my skin, and my shoes are showing holes. I'm sporting a long, unruly beard, resembling a caveman. My hair is gray with dust, crowning my head like a snow crust. My teeth are dark yellow, rotting slowly in their sockets. I stink, but no one can smell me, for the blood screams louder. For a fleeting moment, I smelled good, but that was only when the perfume shops in the nearby market were bombed.

The heat is oppressive, scorching, stoking fires upon the fires. The day gives no shelter, and the night no relief. The sun and the relentless bombing have baked the earth a dusty brown. Standing in the blazing sunshine, soaked in my own sweat, I try to cool my heart on memories of cold treats. My mind harks back to the ice-cream trucks of childhood, roaming the streets with loud blaring music, and I find the memory so heartwarming I nearly drown in my own sweat. Fires without, and fires within! Our skies are constantly on fire—no wonder our food is often overcooked. Sometimes, when the unending bombing turns the place a hell of perpetual fire, the earth heats up to an unbearable cauldron, so unbearable you could fry an egg in the open air, if only those eggs existed!

I remember the cold slushy smoothies of childhood, abounding with strawberries, oranges, and watermelons, which thrived here once. Or the warm ones! There was a native beverage, a cold winter delight, made of milk pudding and adorned with cinnamon and nuts, creamy, foamy, sweet in your mouth, warm in your heart. Those were good times, heedless and happy, upended only by war and this unending siege, which seems to linger and linger, with no end in sight.

Some moments shall not go unremembered. I'm speaking of the outburst of unrestrained joy that has swept the camp as the trucks boom forward, promising life and an end to our suffering, which has lingered beyond endurance. But we can see the end now. We can see the rainbow in the clouds, the sun on the horizon, glowing like a burning loaf of flatbread in a stone oven! And we can all rejoice, yes—we are not ashamed of rejoicing over a bowlful of flour, the real shame is to deprive us of this most ancient human good in the name of civilization! We can all rejoice, oh yes, for we have suffered and endured bravely, and joined together by a bond of shared suffering that has spared no one, like an imagined community of sufferers: The withered children to whom the taste of bread has become a distant memory. The walking dead come to life as if resurrected by the sheer promise of flour. The hapless parents who have sat and watched in dreadful mortification as their little ones petered away. The old men who have morphed into shells of their former selves, with nothing but a long white beard as the last witness to their old age. The men and women who have suffered and endured in silence, not because they did not wish to scream out in pain, but because the pain has dulled their voices, as if frozen in a state of oppressed silence. The poor animals walking among us like bone-dry scarecrows, their bodies thinned out by hunger, and their mighty bellies depressed into frightening hungry holes. The dogs that no longer recognize themselves as dogs, and the cats that have forgotten how to meow. That was the fate of my cat, my furry companion. I adopted her from the street in the last war, and for a good long while, we were quite inseparable. Poor thing starved and shriveled quietly away, and died in my arms without so much as a moan. And if that was the fate of the seemingly immortal cats, with their seven souls, imagine the children!

But the children are astonishingly resilient, which humbles the pain of older souls. Images of displaced children pulling cats from the rubble have made me cry. It's delicate enough to pull someone from the rubble in one piece, where oftentimes you need to dig with your bare hands lest you pull the poor thing apart; now imagine pulling out a cat with nothing left but bare bones and a furry coat that's clearly torn out. But the sight of terrified cats ducking under rubble is also haunting, for even in their frightened and petrified state, our furry companions still look frightening. Their cries make your skin crawl. And imagine when the cat, long stranded under rubble, comes out at last, reduced to a feline skeleton by prolonged hunger and thirst, gazing at people through a pair of hollow and baffled eyes, like a haunting ghost!

Yet the children remain remarkably spirited, subsisting on wonderfully little hope. One child stands waiting with his empty bowl, seeming utterly happy, and I can swear that I have never seen such joy on a human face before. He has lost half of his body's weight, one gathers from his diminished frame, but he seems grateful for the remaining half. It's a miracle that he can stand unaided. But he does, and does it bravely, like a shriveled tree in a harsh winter.

My heart goes out to the little girl with the princess dress, which seems to have widened on her from prolonged hunger. If hunger were a man, I would have killed him and danced on his corpse! She seems to be on her own, for no one is accompanying her. But she's hardly alone, as most children here are unaccompanied, fetching for themselves in this manmade jungle. Yet she seems to take her pain lightly—or perhaps she retains no memory of it, being too young to remember or fathom her loss—for when a stranger offers her an empty bowl, her little face, rimmed with dirt and dust, beams into a wide smile, then she gladly takes her place in the breadline as if queuing for a carousel ride.

She reminds me of Baby Angel, whose surviving miracle is now the talk of the camp. Nameless, days old, and desperately thin, she was found by rescuers in a tree in the vicinity of her family's house, which was bombed to its foundation. They say she was flung into the branches by the same blast that killed the rest of her family. Born unnamed, rescuers christened her Baby Unknown. Judging from her umbilical cord, she was one day old when she was rescued. People believe she was hidden there by an angel, hence her new name: Angel. Her story is that of thousands of wounded children with no surviving family—nameless little angels in a godless world. Or consider the ordinary miracle of the wretched baby girl who was saved with a knife from the womb of her wounded mother, who lay bleeding for hours and survived just long enough to deliver the miracle. Orphaned upon arrival, she entered this world motherless, with nothing but a name tag around her wrist bearing the name of her dead mother. No miracle is ever perfect here, for the parents often need to die for you to survive or be saved.

I stand there pondering what's more tragic: When the parents die and leave the children behind in this godforsaken hell, or when the children die and the parents are left to grieve. No wonder families now wish to die together; you see them waiting in constant embrace under relentless bombardment. That's the natural order of things. Chronology is not just a linear necessity but an existential condition. A father should never outlive his children. A father who outlives his children is a dead father. My father, praise be, was never afraid of death, only of outliving us. In his reckoning, death was the beginning, a magic carpet that would fly him away from his miseries to a better place, a kinder land, a heaven of eternal happiness. Happy are the faithful! To confess, I had always feared dying before my parents, for I was ashamed and mortified at the prospect of their grief, because if I died, my father's tears would shame me, even in my grave.

It's humanly impossible to picture yourself in the place of a father sitting helpless before his starving child, hanging there powerless while hunger eats his precious one away. No father should outlive his child that way. My father believed it and acted on it. Providing for your children, putting food on the table, is fatherhood's most sacred mission, and it has been taken away from us to rob us of our sacred paternity, shame us before our children, and *dehumanize* us in the eyes of humanity. It's not for nothing that we call our men breadwinners and bread givers, for that's what nature has intended them to do. I remember my father in those days of deprivation, a hapless patriarch with five empty mouths to feed, five hungry souls gaping at an empty table, pleading with mouths agape, like little birds in a nest, and nothing, absolutely nothing, shamed my father as losing his ability to put food on the table. *Buckle down! Buckle down!* was his motto in those times of want, which he repeated to us like holy writ. And down we buckled and tightened our belts until there was hardly any beef left to tighten.

My father labored hard. He moonlighted so we could outshine our enemies, worked his tail off so we could put on wings and fly. "Rise and shine and outshine your enemy," was his motto, which he repeated to us daily. He labored like a mule to put food in our mouths, and he watched us eat with the joy of a benevolent god. An early riser, he never missed a dawn. He got up to pray, toil, and fend for us. The sun was his boon companion, for he left home and returned by it. Our house was a boot camp, and he seldom let us sleep past dawn. He believed that a refugee must rise before humankind to catch up with them. He himself never rested, save to pray. God created Man and then rested, but my old man never did. When I looked into his eyes, I saw that he was tired of eking out this burdensome existence. I smile at the memory of his tall figure coming home from work, tired and spent, shaking off the dust from his person, managing a slightly contorted smile, his face burned by the bright sun. The man toiled for years while I enjoyed the fruits, and just as the first apples ripened, he lucked out and died.

I think of all the poor little ones who withered away and wasted in the arms of their hapless parents. There they lay shrunken and shriveled, eerily diminished, perishing like flowers severed too soon, the skin cleaved to the bones, the arms and hands withered, the bellies swollen like balloons on the verge of explosion, the eyes a pair of deep hollows, the faces lined with deep furrows where the smiles had once been, the whole body as dry as a stick. If only they could wait a day or two longer! If only they could hear the bellows in the distance! If only they could open their dying eyes and glimpse the rainbow on the horizon! If only heaven could intervene in some measure to halt the march of time!

The roars grow louder, mixing with the shouts of children and clatter of empty pots, like a cacophony of church bells that ring the sky on a holiday. Holiday! It gives me chills to think that a holiday past, these wretched children had loving parents, and new clothes, and new toys, and plenty of food to eat! To think that this holiday has come and gone without a bell, hardly a cheer. There is no one left to ring the bells, or beat the drums, or sound the cheers. Even the night criers and drummers, the early risers and lantern bearers who wandered the streets and woke us up before dawn to eat, are gone. But all isn't gloom. Soon the empty bowls will fill up, and bread will be made in plenty, and this whole nightmare will be a memory, like the residue of a bad dream. For one virtue of hunger is that it leaves no visible wounds or scars, though it does dent your soul. The children will forget, the young blank on, and the old die content. Perhaps one day, we will look back at this and manage a sardonic laugh. Let's fill those bowls, and feed the children, and let the pain fade from memory, let time intervene in great measure to assuage and lend an azure tint to it!

It takes no great leap of imagination to picture the sort of melancholic existence people lead in a besieged land where a bowl of flour has become a manna from heaven. You see old men, some toothless, others with rotten, yellowed teeth, stand waiting, shaking their empty bowls with their old, trembling hands, pleading for the last sacrament that never comes, while the cacophony of grumbling hunger and clattering bowls is the sound of a skeleton dance. How sad it is to die old and hungry! My grandmother lived long and died old. She lived a hundred years and outlived a hundred wars and sieges. She survived the Great Famine, and many others. She subsisted on garlic and onion. She cracked bones and sucked their marrow dry and slurped it like some exquisite delicacy. She was a stalwart woman who never broke—made in the image of the homeland, born from the soil, to which she returned. The wrinkles on her face resembled the bark of an old olive tree. She died in the last war. One night, without premonition, she closed her eyes and passed on quietly, without so much as a goodbye. Perhaps she felt too ashamed to live so long when her children were dying in rapid succession.

My grandfather was a child when he was exiled from the old country, *uprooted* like an old olive tree cut off at the roots with nothing left but a scar. I remember him, wearing his traditional scarf, leaning on his cane, fiddling with his worry beads, smiling sometimes, waiting for the peace that never came, and when it did come at long last, it was only on the wings of death. He prayed for peace on Earth, peace in our land, peace to the world. Perhaps he was praying for his own peace. For many years, the old man sat quietly on his doorstep smoking his pipe and waiting for death to come and wash the past away.

He died quietly in his bed, a shameless, leisurely death. Somehow, the sweet whiff of his pipe survives in my memory. He nicknamed me *little ghoul*, to scare my enemies, not knowing that one day I would resemble one. I was five when he died. I remember after he passed on, I went to the cemetery and stood by his grave, waiting for a word, a sign of what had happened to us. There was nothing but dreary silence. He was a coward even in his grave. What had he to fear, now that he was dead?

They must be in heaven now, resting in peace at last. Perhaps not heaven, but surely a better place, a place without walls or borders, a place where people roam free, like sheep on the moor. I remember the day I accompanied my grandfather to shepherd his flock in the open fields, and he snoozed under his fig tree having entrusted his herd to me, and as I started to count the sheep I too dozed off and veered into a world of my own creation, paddling away into my paradisial reveries while the real world slowly receded, and by the time he woke from his midday snooze the sheep had gone. The sheer memory of my grandfather, screaming in the wake of his flock, draws a rare smile on my weary face.

The panopticon is shrinking on its prisoners. From the perspective of dazzled aliens gazing down on us, our tragedy may seem like a mass hunger strike by mad prisoners. For how could you possibly explain to those bewildered spectators from outer spaces that in our enlightened human century, starvation is still a weapon, deployed against a whole people in the name of civilization? How to explain to our extraterrestrial observers that collective punishment is still a thing in these modern times? How to explain to the mystified aliens that human progress is more regressive than linear, that history marches in epochal lapses, and before we know it, humanity reverts to the Stone Age? At least the monkeys did not kill their kind or fight among themselves. They must be watching us, our furry ancestors, rolling and laughing with bemused amazement at our marvelous evolution! And why blame the gloating apes when history in her solemn page informs us that humanity will most likely never advance past the jungle stage? For centuries, they have labored to elevate themselves above it, only to fall headlong into savagery. Remember the ancient king who was condemned to an eternity of futile labor by rolling a heavy rock up and down a high mountain without aim? Excuse my occasional outbursts of emotion, but it's been proven that hunger is the best fodder for anger, and in my state of dark rage and fury, I feel I'm more likely to die from extreme irony than from starvation.

Hunger is a time bomb ticking inside you. For even amid the flour euphoria, you still see parents in the throes of madness, dashing about in frantic hysteria to fetch food for their little ones, like mad hounds hunting for their waiting pups. How can we possibly explain to the little ones that help is on the way? How can we communicate these glad tidings to the dying little animals that seem not to understand this human drama? Even the big cats of the local zoo have given up the fight and withered into bare skeletons. The wild beasts have dwindled into the most wretched state imaginable, walking among us so meekly, and seeming, fortunately, too powerless to eat us alive. Even the mighty horses have perished and lucked out, and if that was the fate of mighty horses, imagine the little souls whose tender bones have broken clear out of their skin. Take it from us, Sapiens, the next war will not be a space war, but one pitting hunters against gatherers! It won't be fought with smart bombs or suicide drones, but with sticks and axes.

One can already perceive hints of humanity's future in the skirmishes that break out here on occasion and threaten to escalate into a brother's war over a truckload of flour. Nothing terrifies a starving people awaiting aid as much as the dreadful prospect of looting. People revert to the laws of the jungle, where only the strong survive, while the weak trample underfoot without so much as a howl. It's not unprecedented in these quarters to see a perfectly peaceful breadline morph into a warzone at the speed of fire. Already, I can glimpse wolves forming into packs, waiting on tenterhooks, with bloodshot eyes and flexed arms, jostling and shoving their way through the crowd, shouldering past the weak and the meek, and thrashing you in the process and making you spin on your axis without so much as looking back to see if you are still alive. Or perhaps it's my paranoid mind speaking, for that's what hunger does to you, it blunts your faith in humans and makes you mistrust your own flesh! For the truth is that the people are too battered and feeble to shoulder any burden weighing more than a bowl of flour, let alone a sack of flour. They can barely hold themselves upright. If they have a fragment of vigor left, they would do well to spare it to rebuild their rubble homes and upended lives, and shore up those fragments against their ruins.

As I make my way through a sea of starved people, I see the girl, thinned out by prolonged hunger and destitution, standing there with her empty bowl, waiting. She has dark hair the color of night, but twice as dark, broken in places by lightly deployed henna shades. Her olive eyes look tired and dusted, slightly sleepy, but otherwise warm and gleaming; flecked with amber and rimmed with kohl, the most beautiful eyes under the eastern sun. They gaze straight into your soul, piercing your heart unknowningly and without so much as looking back to see what they have wreaked in their wake. Her weak smile is disarming and would melt stone. She has a freckled face to boot, which pairs well with her strong features and sunny demeanor. For all the hunger and exhaustion, a glimmer of former beauty is still visible in her. The brown dusty dirt across her face only enhances the beauty of her large oval eyes, which gleam faintly in the sun. Like two oases in the desert, they beckon you to follow them down the fire. For all the dust she's gathered on the road, there is no mistaking the beauty mark on her upper cheek; it sits there almost invisible, discernible only to the most enchanted. She has a proud nose besides, like the race that hatched her. Made in her people's image, as they say. A hint of her dignified demeanor is visible in the way she walks.

The open sea roars beyond the harbor breakers, and the fresh onshore wind caresses her face with gentle strokes, mixing with wisps of sunlight. Paired with her beautiful face, her hennaed hair resembles a moonlit night. For modesty's sake, she has plaited it in braids beneath a black-and-white scarf adorned with floral motifs. What betrays her beauty are those thin plaits that emerge from under the scarf, spreading freely on her shoulders, like windblown feathers, gently uncurling with the blows of a breeze and the winds of passage. She strikes me as bashful, which in these quarters is a sign of beauty.

For a precious moment, I forget about my pain, and a new hunger takes hold, an emotional one, a new sort of yearning, a new craving. My heart pounds violently in my chest, and I lose myself in the thrill of this novel emotion, which now threatens to overtake me. A dash of nameless passion runs through my red veins, a newborn desire. But no! Hunger is fatal to love. No romance can flourish in this hell. Love is nonexistent here, dead upon arrival. No one can love on an empty stomach, trust me. You need guts to rip open your heart and offer it to someone. When did you ever hear of romance blooming in a food line? What have I done to deserve her? What have I got to offer her? No red roses ever bloom here, and no hearts flourish, nothing but broken hearts, broken dreams, and broken promises. Dreams are not meant for the hungry, for one must be asleep to believe in them, and no one sleeps on an empty stomach. You will be amazed at how many romances have bloomed and floundered under these grim skies, which rain nothing but death. There is a wedding, a brief honeymoon, and a couple murdered in their fleeting happiness, like a pair of roses plucked too soon. It all happens in a blur, like a sudden thunder, which can be a blessing when you think about it. Away, love, begone! And even yet love and happiness still sprout in this doomed place, yes, like wild weed through the rocks. This morning, I could hear a wedding proceeding amid the ruins. You could hear the ululations, the sound of rice beating on the red grounds, and see the smoke of the incense rising to usher the happy couple into marriage. Or perhaps it was all in my hopeful imagination.

Perhaps these joyful shrills are mere echoes from the past; a voice from kinder and happier days. My mother was a ululator of the first rank. She liked to sing, and no power on Earth could stop her when she crooned on. She had a warm voice, especially in the winter, when the rain howled outside. It was softer than the rain, and calm as a midsummer breeze. She sang beautiful love poems, to lift her spirit and keep it from dissipating. She owned a sewing machine that worked magic. It clanked and rumbled tirelessly, while she sat there singing, bittersweet songs of the beautiful life she never had. In my delirium of pain, I see a young woman swinging and lulling her sleepless child to sleep, rocking his little bed to the rattle of rockets, singing: *Sleep, my sweet little bird!*

My mother was an ordinary woman living in extraordinary times. I see her as a goddess, ageless in her absence, younger in my memory. She was a beautiful girl once. I know this because a vestige of that beauty was always visible in her. I can picture her in days of youth, washing her young feet in the Mediterranean, dreaming of marriage and romance, indulging in romantic visions of the future. She was passionate, volatile, and quick to anger, and I stirred her rage into a froth. She was eerily peaceful in her better days. But come the war, she was like a wild bear robbed of her cubs. She loved me, for that was all she could afford in her state of abject dispossession. It took her dying for me to be touched by the depth of her affection. I do miss my mother, yes, though I hardly remember what it's like to have one. I feel lonely without her, a motherless cub besieged by a pack of starving lions roaring for his blood. In the dead of night, her face comes alive, and with it the memory of all the times she sat by my bed, comforting me, singing her ageless melodies. I can feel the touch of her comforting hands reaching out to me from the grave. I resist a powerful desire to weep. And fancy my astonishment when I suddenly realize that my girl, with her freckled face and oval eyes and strong features, bears an uncanny resemblance to my mother!

Imagine my utter dismay when I glimpse myself in a broken mirror on the road, and see a creature nearly reduced to bare bones, looking like half the man he was before. He resembles a bare vine shoot sucked dry of its juices, a tree hollow teetering about in a state of dreamless hallucination. His flesh is wasting away, his skin shriveling. Inflamed and heated from hunger's rage, his body feels like an oven. His face is caving in, and his features darkened, his eyes white with horror and despair, for he can feel the terror of starvation in his ravaged body. All the flour in the world will not restore this creature to a wholesome human being. Who would marry me in this condition? Can I hold my beautiful bride in my arms and show her the red flowers in the sky? I would faint on the altar. There is no altar; the bombing has flattened this place. One is lucky to have a toehold of solid ground underfoot. There is no altar here but the one gazing upon us—the sacrificial lambs bleating in silence and dying without ceremony.

I remember when I was a schoolboy, there was an eerie-looking, human-like skeleton in our biology lab; we liked to poke fun at it, not knowing that we would be next. For I have seen my old pals, and it's not a pleasant sight. At least I'm still in one piece, mainly. I have noticed that many of the children waiting are missing hands or legs, which they likely lost to the bombs. They are visibly struggling with their empty bowls, which seem to weigh them down. Luckily, flour is light and has low density, though its effect can be magical. Our land produced flour in plenty once, but since our besiegers destroyed the grain mills, burned down the wheat fields, poisoned the water wells and basins, blew up the local bakeries, bombed the soup kitchens, food carts, and marketplaces, slayed the vendors, and wiped out the millers, flour has vanished. We sowed our wheat and ate bread by the sweat of our brow, before the bombs rained down and the land was scorched beyond redemption.

They say that our earthbound people, who resemble the color of earth, can hardly be distinguished from the soil when laid in the ground. But that's all history now, the stuff of national lore and nostalgia, a paradise lost. For now, we must depend on aid flour for survival, which has yet to come. For months, this tiny strip of land has been under a total blockade, with no way in, no way out, and no end in sight. No one ventures and stays alive. Yet one can hardly stay alive without venturing out. To stoke our loss, they burned the olive groves and let the people watch it.

It was a sad sight, watching our olive groves, the seeds of our ancestors, burn to ashes. Whole acres of natural beauty have vanished into thin air! Many have been uprooted. You see old people, clinging madly to the ancient trees while the heartless bulldozers approach, pleading to die along with their trees. I remember the look on my father's face when the soldiers razed his olive grove to build a border wall. He stood there silently and watched as a fleet of wheeled crawlers tore his orchard apart. All was gone, paradise lost. That land was his heart, his *raison d'être*, his belonging, his emblem of rootedness. I shall never forget his face as he knelt on the ground and clung to the last olive tree, hanging onto it like a child to his favorite toy, before the soldiers tore him away. He died that day. Surely, he would live to witness the siege that followed, but he was dead within.

Olive oil is our national beverage. We take pride in it. It's our national dessert, especially during the olive season, at the mill, when the oil comes out, hot and green. My favorite dessert was olive oil and sugar spread on flatbread. Some would add honey, which was a luxury. Or jam, which they smuggled through the tunnels, because it's banned here. I hear some managed to smuggle in chocolate, which must've been a rumor. They say it's not wise to consume chocolate under siege. It's a recipe for thirst, they say, which is a bad diet, for water is rare here. It rains seldom, and even when it rains, rainwater is forbidden to us, and woe to those who venture to collect it! Seawater too, hence our food is undersalted. The sea is less than a hundred feet away, and our food is undersalted! Salt is sacred here. In happier and kinder times, we used it to preserve meat in the fashion of our ancestors, especially after the hospitals were bombed and refrigerators repurposed as morgues. Now we apply it to preserve the corpses. Which perhaps explains why people here would perish of hunger sooner than eat refrigerated food. Sugar is scant too. When they first invaded, the soldiers set fire to the beehives, burning whole colonies of them to ashes. Fields blazing with flowers went up in flames. They say sugar stimulates our people and makes the children happy, and nothing pains our besiegers like seeing our children happy. Condiments of aphroditic quality are banned too, for they arouse sexual desire and encourage reproduction, and nothing agonizes our oppressors like seeing us procreate and grow in numbers. It's like a demographic war to them. It's not a fairytale that our men smuggle sperm out of prison camps to have children and raise families. Many of us have been conceived that way.

A sudden unslakable thirst takes over me as I entertain those thoughts, and I pass out, roaming dreamlike in a desert of deprivations—my life under siege.

Nothing was left, and no one was spared. The people who once fed these quarters have been mowed down. The butchers butchered. Cooks bombed with chilling precision. Bakers burned alive. There was an old baker who delivered bread to our camp every day at dawn. He had visible burns on his body, mainly his face, but he was as punctual as the sun. He died in the first bombing, which hit his bakery with deadly precision. Nothing remained of him but the ashes of what was once a full-fledged human being. Of the place, nothing was left but ashen ruins. Even the little birds that clustered about the bakery could not escape the maw of death. And those were not the only birds to perish that way. Remember the rooftop bird coops, kept for generations? They were the first to go. Even the bird feeders, which our parents built in their peaceful days, were bombed! And this *was* a peaceful place once, briefly, so peaceful a bird could land on your shoulder and pick the food crumbs off your shirt, and feel perfectly at peace. There were no bombs pouring down oblivious to the havoc they were about to wreak. Or warplanes whooshing overhead, ready to rain on us with the latest innovations of human evil, which never ceases to amaze. Those giant fiery birds rise from the ground as would a phoenix from its ashes, piercing the sky like snorting dragons, breathing fire and spreading death and destruction—and *boom*, all is gone! One moment, you are a human being with grand dreams and hopes, the next, you are crushed under rubble like a dead rat.

Speaking of rats, have you ever eaten one? No, it's not on our national menu, and by no means a local delicacy. I'm speaking of eating rats to survive. You shut your eyes, hold your nose, and guzzle it down swiftly. The taste is so strong you must pair it with spices. And plenty of sea salt, for it has a cleansing effect. And wash it down with water, of course. It takes guts to eat a dead rodent. But not all rodents are created equal. There is the black rat, the brown rat, and the house mouse. And the blind mole rats, which haunt the mountains. And the fat sand rats, which are found in plenty in the desert, and abound in these quarters. And if you have gone this far, perhaps you would want to consider the snakes, which are more edible than rats, but can be poisonous if not properly cooked. And good luck hunting these most elusive creatures!

Hunger reveals a new species in you, a gnawer you never knew existed. You discover that the human will to survive is boundless and limitless, like a monstrous, serpentine, multi-headed hydra with multiple lives and unlimited levers. How do you suppose our ancestors survived the locust invasion, when swarms of locusts invaded these quarters and covered the sky like a dark blanket, amassing in such density they eclipsed the sun, gnawing at everything that sprouted on the ground, devouring everything green, even the bark of trees, while laying their eggs in great plenty, ready to hatch young insects that would march in long columns and feed on whatever was left, before leaving the land wholly ravaged in their wake?

The siege is the locust plague of our time, except it's human-made, imposed on us by a vindictive force that can never be made to understand what hunger does to our souls. They do it, and celebrate it, and find no one among them to condemn it. And even then, you can still eat the locusts, but can you eat your oppressor's flesh? Perhaps only in your famished imagination. Give me a starving soul in these depleted quarters who does not yearn to eat the flesh of his oppressors, or pray that his oppressors shall eat their own flesh and drink their own blood as wine!

But we shall not resort to such extreme measures. For now, more than ever before, we can hear the trucks crawling, slowly but surely, in our direction. We can hear it and swear to it. You must remember that we are good listeners. Blame it on our unending scramble for survival. War after war, we have acquired astonishing survival instincts that would turn bats and owls green with envy. There is hardly a sound in these godforsaken quarters we can't make out. We can hear the chirping of crickets and the creeping of beetles in the leaves. While it ravages your body, hunger can sometimes sharpen your senses. Your sense of hearing is astonishingly acute, wholly attuned to the rumbles on the road, or the whistles of ships at sea, which soon die out in the whirl of bombing. But you hear it all, for the moment you stop hearing it, you are probably dead.

For all the glaring hope, and despite the raging flour euphoria, a blazing guilt takes hold of me—a fit of inevitable regret that has swelled into self-pity. I always saluted myself for staying out, for defying exile and resisting being uprooted to my last breath. But now, having touched the limits of my endurance, I wish I left this hellscape when I had the chance, when I was strong and had fight in me, when my feet could take me far and away. I always dreamed of escape, flying over these border walls on my magic wings. Or boarding a refugee boat and sailing away wherever the winds took me, never to return—like my displaced ancestors who took to the sea and vanished. What ailed me, what *possessed* me not to run away? Was I too cowardly to flee, to pack my old life in a bundle and leave the only place I call home? Was I afraid to vanish at sea, to be swallowed by a large fish like the good prophet of yore? How spineless of me!

Perhaps when this nightmare ends, I will marry that girl, and we will flee together to a kinder place, a land where newlywed lovers outlive their honeymoon and live happily ever after, and maybe even proceed to make children with plenty to eat! Please don't let our destitute state fool you, for we are more romantic than we let on. Tough as nails on the outside, but tender within. We pine and yearn like all people, though we rarely admit it. Our love is deep and austere. My parents were poor and young, and all they could afford was solemn romance. How do you suppose I was brought into this world? Legend says that he made her a wedding bed out of a dead olive tree, where I was conceived and sprang to life. They loved and suffered each other in silence. They were so fatally in love they died together in the first bombing. They died in each other's arms, quite suitably, as if satisfied they came to a most fitting end. They never traveled apart on Earth, and there was no reason why they should journey to heaven apart. Oh, heaven, for shame, how many sorrows we unload at your threshold! It amazes me that for the infinite degeneracy of humankind, there's still room in that heaven. Are they looking down on me? Surely they are not smiling, seeing me in this miserable condition.

Sometimes I wish to die sooner, to be united with them, but then I remember a promise I made to my father to stay alive. Or perhaps it's in my human nature—the desire to stay alive cannot be sacrificed for a distant image of heaven and eternal happiness. One must not belittle this human desire to survive and live and outlive death itself—a desire so great it rivals eternity and makes heaven roil in its boredom. I will wait, thank you. Eternity be damned! And what is life but a fleeting sojourn on Earth thrust randomly between two eternities?

As I hang there entertaining these fateful thoughts, I meet a child who sits hiding behind a bulldozer's wheels, sweating and trembling from cold and fear, his face blue, his eyes sunken, his body a mere frame of bones. He's hoping to die under wheels, he tells me in his trembling voice, to reunite with his family in heaven. I lend him a hand and walk him to the shelter, where he dies shortly after. I console myself with the thought that he has not died alone. A soothing thought suddenly takes hold of me: There's one thing worse than dying in this grand crucible of war and starvation, and that's dying in exile, alone and unremembered, thousands of miles away from your dear old homeland, the land of your ancestors, where you sowed your first seeds and stole your first kiss. The thought takes root when I remember the girl with the freckled face, oval eyes, and strong features. Already, I can feel the first stirrings of love in my belly, and with them, a new resolve to stay put and steadfast, and survive. These red grounds are not done speaking, and so long as yearning is concerned, there remains more love in these sad quarters than in the loveless plains of exile. Give me the sea, sight of memories and desires! The sad red oranges, bleeding, ripening in the warm sun! The olive trees, older than the soil in which they stand! The people, my poor humble people who expect nothing, and who for all the misery remain hopeful and steadfast.

People are waiting with shattered nerves, their patience wearing thin, and their bodies thinner. It's doubtful there is flour for everyone, but we will share what destiny has to offer. When it's wartime, you accept whatever comes to you. We have no guards or custodians or law keepers to speak of, for few have survived the bombing, so we rely on people to follow the moral order of things: Children first, then women, then old men, and young ones last. It's the *natural* order of things. Or at least that's how the people hail it. So far as hunger is concerned, children always come first. The little ones have suffered plenty, and can wait no more. They look frightful in those bloated bellies, filled with air and water, motionless features, and grotesquely protruding ribs. Hunger has hollowed their faces, cheeks, and eyes, eating away at them like an insatiable worm. Reduced to bone surfaces, diminished to a frame, stripped of flesh, their skin hangs in ghastly folds. They seem too weak to stand upright or walk among us, too mortified by their own appearance to draw attention to themselves. They see things dimly, like phantoms, or faint shadows of color. They are hard of hearing and speaking, and they appear to have lost their voices. Perhaps they never had a voice, born under siege and all. Lucky for them, there is a special place in the front row for the newly orphaned, and the newborns, and the nearly dead, those old ghouls living on borrowed time, who will likely not live long after, but at least they will die with dignity.

We may be stateless, but we are not lawless. Our lives are not, as many outsiders believe, nasty, short, and brutish. We are people of substance, affluent in our humble way, and we eat according to our needs. In matters of earthly pleasures, we are quite undemanding, happy with little, modest, and temperate to a fault. Give us bread, and we will survive on the four primary elements that make life possible: Earth, water, fire, and air. Give us bread—or more precisely, stop depriving us of our daily bread, given to us by this most generous of lands.

The line wonderfully holds, and it amazes me that people can remember and uphold the customs in the bleakest of times, demonstrating exemplary patience. But etiquette is etiquette, as they say. Or as my father would say, "Say your prayers, eat with your right hand, from your side." He revered bread like it was manna from heaven. "Bread is your best spoon," he would instruct. "You tear out a mouthful, fold it, curve it, scoop, and dig in." Starved, I've come to appreciate his prayer "May God perpetuate the blessing of food," which in hindsight was more than just spirituality. Prayer often exhibits our deepest fears, and what could be more frightful than hunger?

A rush of nostalgia sweeps over me as a young man standing amid the crowd starts juggling empty bowls to amuse the kids. My mind harks back to those seasonal feasts, with cooks juggling festive bowls of rice and meat and the orphans sitting in the first rows, and before you knew it, the whole camp was fed to the last soul. No chore did I enjoy as a kid more than helping set the table for a holiday feast or a sunset banquet, where I would juggle the dishes to safety while my brothers fought around the big table. It was a prison without warders, our old house. I smile at the memory of those days—five little rascals fighting over a morsel of meat, from hunger, or the sheer fun of it, or perhaps lack of etiquette.

Gazing into the waiting masses, an eschatological image takes hold: There is the hell within the gates, the heaven beyond, and the limbo in which we stand. One feels like hanging on the edge of a cliff, with hell on either side. For heaven is a mere fantasy, a fairytale invented to comfort the little children who die of hunger and destitution. For those still clinging to life, there is the hell within, and the hell without, and the one thereafter, and little else. Nothing awaits survivors but pain and misery, and a loss too great to comprehend. For the truth is that survival is marginally preferable to death in this wasteland. When starving, you are busy eking out your fragile survival in this human jungle, but once full and content, once the fires within have been put out, you will be brought face to face with your loss and the inevitable reckoning that lies in store and quietly awaits you, and before long, a new torment sits in, and soon you will find yourself in a whole new hell. Our people call it the eternal return of the same.

Time is ticking by; every hour matters. A human tragedy of biblical proportions is about to unfold, and there's but one way to prevent it. Who knew that a powder so plain and versatile, and riddled with germs, could spare a nation! Perhaps there is a kernel of truth in the belief that we are created from flour.

The relentless bombing shows no signs of abating. But people remain resilient, for when hunger overtakes you, your mind can only perceive one facet of survival, and that's survival in the most biological sense of the word. You are too consumed by the fires within to mind the ones without. Sometimes you try to imagine life after flour, or reminisce about the one you once had, but your feeble mind soon gives in and loses itself in the rumble.

You stand in the line, or slightly out of it, but you never allow the trucks to move out of your line of sight. You center your gaze, and lend your ears, and listen to your heart pound faintly in anticipation, while your body threatens to collapse from exhaustion. But you hold out, because to do otherwise would mean surrender. For outsiders, who can never feel your pain or know your story, you are merely a number, the stuff of philanthropic intrigue, a burden, a nausea, a bit player in the unfolding human drama, an extra in the grand global show. To really grasp what it means to be a starving refugee in a swarming breadline, imagine a strip of sand on an abandoned beach on a midwinter day. Each grain of sand is a nameless speck among countless others, but every grain has its own origin and story. Yet when the great storm thunders ashore and sweeps away the sand, all that is personal and unique merges into one tragic, inexorable whole.

And you wait, and hold firmly to your place in the endless line, your senses sharpened, insofar as one can sharpen his senses in this state of utter deprivation. The oppressive heat makes your head feels like a mine threatening to explode, though you feel more lightheaded than otherwise. There is a constant throbbing and aching, accompanied by intermittent blurring and brief eclipsing of vision. There's a certain rot in your soul, but your body is too tormented to bother with it.

I'm extremely hungry. My stomach has shrunk to the size of an olive—a peewee pouch dry and shriveled, and sore as a hot wound. And besides hunger, I'm thirsty as a desert, dehydrated like a stray dog. My throat is dried out, and my mouth shriveled as withered tumbleweed. I feel exhausted and worn out. I haven't slept for days and nights. Who sleeps with hunger? That monster never sleeps or lets you sleep. There are no sheep left to count, as the locals say. Funny, these people! They have a saying for everything. Give them a thread, and they will weave a good yarn from it. I'm looking dirty besides; frankly, I *reek*. I haven't showered for weeks. My teeth are yellowed, my feet bare, my face ashen with the smoke of war, and my body battered from constant survival. For if you survive the bombs, you might as well die of fatigue, the relentless charade of escaping death. Many of us have perished that way. Others merely faint from sheer exhaustion and pass to a better place, where there is no hunger. Or so we believe.

A sense of nameless despair takes over me when I contemplate our life after flour. Because once you are full and content, once your biological needs have been adequately fulfilled, existential worries take hold. The war has left nothing standing. If we survive, what do we survive for? There's nothing left, no family, no house, and no shelter. Even the tents have burned to the ground. The place as we knew it no longer exists, or perhaps exists merely as a monochrome of its former glory. Even the landscape has been erased, cleansed like erased markers on a map. It's been firebombed, reduced to dust and rubble, resembling the surface of the moon. The Beach Road, once the pride of the coast, the road that mapped the happy venues of my youth, is no more. A long stretch of dirt, dark, and gray, now looms ghostlike where the road once passed. Life has ceased to exist here, if by life you mean something beyond bare existence.

My mood is excited, and beyond the excitement, there is the inevitable sense of melancholy, the feeling of someone who has lost everything, and all that's left to him is a dreamless wish to fetch a bowl of flour to keep himself alive. It appears to me that the undignified excitement and thrill of mere human survival is inescapable, even when it means a bowl of flour to preserve you and shove that monster away, and however fleeting that survival may prove to be. Let my last sight be not over the promised land, but a freshly baked piece of flatbread! Let the hardy women of this land bake it in plenty and feed the dying children of the motherland, the little souls who were born and raised in this manmade jungle!

Imagine our collective dismay when we learn that our besiegers, out of sheer malice, evidently, have limited our aid convoy to one truck! One lone truck—how many famished souls can a truckload of flour feed? Hardly a camp, let alone a strip of land stranded between desert and sea and swollen by the displaced! This act of pure malice—for there is no other word to describe it—this unhinged malevolence could trigger a civil war, a brother's war over flour, from which no soul would emerge alive, except maybe the wolves, and the vultures, which are circling over us, ready to swoop down and devour us to the last corpse.

People are starving to death. You can hear their bellies growl. They drink seawater, cook tree leaves, and eat grass and animal food for survival. Women grind fodder to mimic baking flour. People would trade gold for flour if they could find any. Surely you heard of the man who sold his wife's dowry, only to realize that his money is no good in these besieged quarters! What good is gold in a place where nothing glimmers but the sure glint of death? But hunger, they say, is a recipe for desperation. One father has offered to sell his good kidney to feed his family. Oh, the drama of human frailty is unrivaled! What good are kidneys in this place of destitution? Confronted with the insanity of his offer, he points to his chest with dramatic flair, and hollers: "I'd pluck out my heart and feed it to them if they would eat it."

But he's far from alone. There's no shortage of fathers who have gone insane. In fact, it would be easier to sort out the ones who, by some fortunate stroke of luck, have eluded this collective descent into madness, which rips through the camps like raging waves. "My girl is so thin she can be a ballerina dancer," one hapless father quips, before bursting into tears. He looks so frightfully thin himself, I wonder if he's fresh out of a torture camp. And we do hear what happens to our men in those torture camps! The horror they experience there sears the imagination. They starve you and throw a feast before your eyes to torment you, and when you wither away and pass on like a dry fig, they summon the dogs to feast on your bones. Many return, if they ever return, as bare skeletons, with broken bones and permanent scars, hollowed cheeks and eyes, their bodies resembling scaffolding around a condemned building. If you listen closely, you can hear the cracking sound of their bones as they rub together; you wonder by what miracle they managed to traverse those hostile terrains on these frames! Others return muted, having lost their voices due to extreme torture. Men who return from those camps are often shocked to find out that their children and loved ones no longer recognize them. They burst into bitter tears of desperation as they stand before the bewildered kids pleading their fatherhood in the frantic hope of being identified. More often those men return bereft of memory, as if wiped out. I remember one day I came home from school and waiting for me was a strange, bearded man with thick grizzled hair, and a frail body slightly thicker than a bamboo cane. Oblivious to my bewilderment, he approached me with outstretched shriveled arms, and I ran out screaming. It was my father, home from exile.

People hang in the unending queue, reminiscing about gentler times. "I breakfasted like a king," an old man, shrunken and exhausted, laments as we stand waiting, evoking a distant memory of better and kinder days, a memory made even more distant by prolonged hunger.

"Now I'm dying like a dog," he adds after a while, laughing bitterly, and revealing the carp-like mouth of a toothless drooler. He tells of faraway places where dogs are petted and pampered, where people watch the news, and see other people starve somewhere, manage a grin, and proceed to enjoy their supper. "Do you know the good thing about hunger?" he asks me, without particularly waiting for my answer. I shake my clueless head, and he says, with a smile: "It keeps you warm at night." When his grin quickly beams out into hysterical laughter, I realize that one frightful and greatly overlooked aspect of hunger is madness.

The women have their share of insanity. A young mother stands with a scrawny boy resembling a tree branch with a head attached. "If this boy starves any longer, he'll disappear," she tells another woman. The other woman, undecided whether to laugh or weep, points to her little girl, who appears even gaunter than the boy, twice as bony. "Poor thing needs a new dress," she says sobbingly, hinting that the child is thinning out of her dress, "Who will marry her?" A third woman walks up with her twin boys, who appear so frightfully thin you wonder if they are one person split in half. She's afraid to hug them lest they break, she tells the other women. "Don't weigh as much as a pair of chickens," she says through tears. The children appear so scrawny, almost weightless, light as a butterfly; a strong wind could blow them away.

I can't help smiling, though I doubt my face would show it. We are a merry people; it's a shame to see us go mad. You see people in the waiting line, honorable folks in their better days, now in rags, with dusty features, long, unruly beards, yellow teeth, and the saddest faces under the sun. Madness is written all over their faces, sometimes faintly, others in bold letters. I can make out former teachers, former preachers, former landlords, all former respectable men and women of society. Old flames greeting each other with downcast eyes and the inevitable trepidation of being recognized. Children once spoiled and pampered by loving parents, showered with love and gifts, regaled with lavish birthdays, are now newly orphaned, with missing legs and hands, broken bones and hearts, all standing equally in the flour line, holding their empty bowls and pots, waiting. I was a spoiled kid once, briefly, before I was orphaned. I long for the time, and it was a long time ago, when finishing your food was deemed a heroic deed, praiseworthy. I cherish the memory of my mother beseeching me to eat: "If you finish your food, I have a reward for you!" And there was nothing, absolutely nothing, more rewarding than those homemade sweets that delighted the heart and elevated the soul! I wish I had eaten it all when I could.

And to think that these kids, in their better days, would refuse a banana because, pardon me while I laugh, it was a bit mushy, or slightly overripe, or showing brown spots on its peel—to think that these little devils whined about the apple showing wrinkles on the inside, or freckles on the outside, or waxing yellowish in places, and not too fresh, which was perfectly edible, now when you think about it in hindsight. Or those ingrates who moaned that the tomato was too juicy! Now the little rascals, these tortured souls who barely remember what a fruit looks like, would eat the apple with its core, and the banana with its peel, and suck the tomato with its stem, and thank the earth that yielded them. They would eat from the cursed tree in the center of hell if they could get their hands on it. These kids have lost their right to be picky, because there's nothing left to pick, except perhaps their dust-ridden noses. Gone is the time when a kid would look at a perfectly delicious cracker and complain that it was broken in half, that it wasn't whole! Or when presented with a piece of biscuit and protest that it was—grasp the hilarity—a tad crumby! Or when the cracker fell to the floor and was no longer deemed edible. "It touched the floor," they would scream, as if they were not created from dust and dirt, as if they were not born from the soil, as though they had not come from the earth, as if they had come down from heaven! Or when a fresh apple fell to the floor, and they complained that the apple was irrecoverably "bruised," as if our unending human miseries were not a sad consequence of a fallen apple! Or when they accused a perfect bowl of rice of being sticky, or partly crunchy. Or when they claimed that the smoked fish of the local market smelled like a corpse, which it did, to be fair. Or when they lashed at the soup for being a touch lumpy, or a bit watery, and not creamy enough. I bet they regret it now, turning away perfectly edible food for not being quite palatable! Rasping and moaning about a perfect piece of bread. *Insulting* bread! "The bread is a tad soggy!" "The loaf is too bready!" "The cheese has holes!"

Remember when they groaned that grandma's pudding was *boring*? Or when they steamed about the milk for not being foamy or bubbly enough? Or when they griped that the milk was too cold, or too hot, when it was perfectly drinkable at every temperature? For milk is milk, and one needn't starve to death to appreciate this elementary culinary fact. Or when they grumbled that the freshly drawn cow milk, excuse me again, was "too milky," and would not stop until presented with factory milk, which tasted like liquefied powder, remember?

I smile at the memory of my grandmother. I picture her in those days of plenty, milking her cow and making me the richest homemade pudding known to humankind. One day, she was showing me how to milk a cow. It shifted restlessly, and I wept and would not stop until she made me one of those mouth-watering milk puddings that made the children leap in delight. Can we reclaim the past once it has acquired the status of a lost paradise?

This right now is the hungriest place on Earth. Perhaps if we knew it, we would've consumed less and saved more for this rainy day. Perhaps we would've been less generous with poor strangers who once roamed our quarters. Where are they now, those strangers? Our people are mad with generosity; it's sad to see us starve to death. Our ancestors killed their horses to feed a wanderer. So it goes. They kept the fire burning by their tents. Our house is your house, we told strangers, when we still had houses left. Once a stranger is ushered into our homes, he becomes a lucky hostage. We feed him for three days and nights before we let him go. In their unhinged generosity, our people would go hungry to feed a stranger in their midst. Now we are the strangers, and we are starving in your midst, dear humans. But we will not beg, no, because we are a highly dignified people, and it's not in our nature to ask for charity. We will not beg, because it's a forced starvation, imposed on us by a vengeful force that revels in torturing us—because humans are entitled to bread, and it's our right, yes, given to us by the laws of nature and the dictates of shared humanity. Because the moment you weaponized hunger and made it a collective punishment, you didn't triumph over us, but merely descended into barbarism. But we will never beg at your doors, nor accept charity from you. If we plead for human kindness, it's only because the heavens have betrayed us.

Oh, heaven, for shame, how could you, how *dare* you, be so impassive! Even airdropping food from these hostile skies has proven a disaster. It has killed more people than it saved. Most parcels landed deep and far in the sea. Others landed on the heads of waiting children. Children look at the sky, wondering whether it's going to drop bread or bombs, as the two are often dropped simultaneously, to feed and kill, in no particular order. It's demeaning, dropping food that way. Even amid starvation, people have dignity. We may look like zombies, but we are humans, and we demand to be treated humanely.

The breadline has created a sense of collective suffering in the camp, which at least soothes our pain. I remember that before the rumors spread and the breadline formed, I was roaming this empty road aimlessly, and there I witnessed an encounter that has haunted me since: A child approached a stranger with an empty bowl in his hand and tears in his eyes. The stranger made a helpless gesture and walked the boy to a nearby shelter. He will be in better company there. Or so he's told. At least he won't be starving alone, though hunger is a lonely torment, as we say, for it eats silently inside you. I never figured out what has become of the child, but I did learn that people can find solace in collective suffering, which is perhaps one of war's few silver linings.

Flour, that magic dust that makes life possible! I smile at the memory of my mother, bringing bread to life with her kneading, pressing and stretching it with the heels of her sturdy peasant hands, folding it over and rotating it in the air like a juggler, before shaping it into that perfect, elastic, and smooth texture, then watching it rise slowly but surely, as if breathing. "It's resting," she was apt to say when her hungry children shifted restlessly around the magical creature, that goodhearted monster that rose from the ashes and tore into hunger without mercy. Breathing, kneading, pressing, resting—a metaphor for life itself.

Sometimes, when hunger overwhelms me, I close my eyes and devour the dough in my hungry imagination—eat it before it's leavened! Perhaps I overeat a bit, gorge myself more than I can consume—eat like a horse, as mother would say—but I'm excused in doing so, given my sorrowful condition. I was always impatient with hunger. One day, my mother was frying me an egg on the stove. Impatiently, I ventured to check on it, and because I reached only halfway to the stove, I pulled the skillet down to see how the egg was doing, dropping it along with the sizzling oil right onto my face. It burned badly, as you can tell from the egg-like scar on my face. Sometimes, in my starved hallucination, I hear the crackling sound of sizzling oil, and I chase it, believing it leads to her. My mother cooked with love and passion. She cooked in large pots, cooked for a clan, for it was a sin to let the aroma of your food waft into a neighbor's home without sharing it. And the neighbors reciprocated, of course. I would deliver a bowl of hot okra stew to a neighbor and leave with a bowl of carob pudding or pomegranate cake. Except one time, during a holiday, I left a neighbor's house with a bowl of milk pudding, and enchanted by its aroma, and the sweet scent of cinnamon, I dozed off and fell in the middle of the road, cutting my head. I somehow let my blood ooze into the pudding, transforming it, to my mother's brief illusion, into pomegranate pudding.

It amazes me to think that most of my scars have been inflicted by food. I still bear the marks from when I burned my fingers while snatching my mother's burning bread from the stone oven. My whole life is scarred with the unending pursuit of food and the desire to soothe my hunger, a lifetime quest for the holy grail of life.

I brood over those old and warm memories as I duck down from the relentless bombing, which threatens to pulverize us to human dust. And if you survive the bombs, good luck surviving the shrapnel, flying about like wasps. And if you survive these, there's always hunger for you, waiting with that bloody and toothless mouth that can devour a nation and never feel satisfied from the fare.

Someone has died. No, he has not died from a firebomb, for people here rarely "die" in the bombing, but merely vanish, disappear without a trace, as if wiped out. He seems to have swallowed an object resembling food, to which he was likely lured by hopeless desperation, or maybe hallucination. He chewed it in a sort of ecstasy or delirium. Then he started to gag and gasp, causing his eyes to stand out and his legs to spread, before falling to the ground with a miserable thud, where a moment later he died a death of indescribable agony.

Fearing a similar fate, people discard whatever objects they have collected from these hostile grounds. And if you had seen the man taking his last breaths, you would've done the same. For this, right now, is a place where biting a bullet is more than just a passing phrase.

Booby traps abound here and have killed people in plenty. They dot the camp like landmines. The grounds are littered with unexploded bombs, sinister in their yellow markings. They lie strewn across the tumble-down landscape, dotting the road with small explosives that look like toys to the children. Smart bombs resembling food cans are left scattered across the place by amused soldiers to kill starving children. You can sense the monsters lurking dormant and concealed just below, ready to unleash death and terror on the heedless surface. They would pop up like dolphins, wiping out everything that stands nearby. You see a human being walking the surface, and then *boom*—he vanishes, with hardly a trace, save for shreds of body parts flying over the surface. It's not a pleasant sight, especially if you happen to be waiting in a food line, though it does have the advantage of putting you off food briefly. Or when the hospitals are bombed, and people keep the dead bodies in food refrigerators and ice-cream trucks! When this very morning, a farmer opened a refrigerator in which he had stored vegetables and fruits, revealing corpses of children and women lying on top of each other, all soaked in blood and bombed beyond recognition, with only a few wrapped in white burial shrouds, people swore on their dear lives that they would die sooner than touch ice cream or any food previously refrigerated.

People wait in fraught anticipation, holding their empty bowls, keeping their eyes downcast, saying little to each other. They stand drifting in a state of awful delirium, shifting like windblown sky dancers. Now and then, worn out by hunger and exhaustion, and mounting frustration, people would lose themselves in a fit of violent rage, throwing tantrums, cursing fate, damning life, praising death. For that is what hunger does to you; it stirs your rage to a simmer and lets you boil on your internal embers, and like feeble steam, you hang there seething in a stew, feeling on the verge of exploding, yet too weak to do so. You curse fate, and find it soothing. But you know it's not fate that's starving us. You know there is no fate but what we make ourselves. It's a mere ruse, a placebo, a comfortable rack on which we hang our pain. Our besiegers are acting like the wrathful gods of yore, dispensing judgment, dealing out life and death by the mere act of laying siege, a primitive and most primordial punishment meted out to a whole people. If destiny did truly exist, then why does she never show her face? How did it come to pass that all the forces that control our lives are faceless and invisible?

I entertain these fateful thoughts as the rumble of wheels fades away in the distance, and the charging trucks slow to a crawl, and every faint quiver of hope dies out quickly. Our besiegers are playing a game of fatal suspense with us, a game of life and death. They are mocking us to death, yes, and they find it bemusing. Perhaps they revel in the sight of our deprivation. Perhaps they delight in the spectacle of our slow and agonizing death. Perhaps they find it droll, to sit and enjoy their seaside view and watch a tide of hungry people ebb and flow, and hit the breakers—a mass of starving men and women, honorable people in their better days, standing with empty bowls and empty bellies, sunbeaten faces, ashen and dusty, and hair graying before its time, huddled together in this manmade cage like sheep in a pen, and dying the most exotic death! What a pleasure to behold the sight of noble savages scrambling for the bread that never comes!

The news has sent ripples of shock through the camps, and people cast their empty bowls on the ground in desperation, howling in despair at their assured fate, their faces blanched with nameless horror, and you needn't see it to know its color. If there is justice in this world, there will be no walls, no gates, nor aid trucks. There will be food for everyone, bread and flour, and cookies to boot. Can anyone tell me what gives a nation the right to besiege another? There are no answers, only clues, wrapped in centuries of human degeneracy. And so all that's solid once again melts into thin air, and our euphoria dwindles to a bleak dissolution.

The suspension of aid is taking its toll on the people. Skirmishes break out and quickly morph into violent bouts, which is comical more than tragic, *tragicomic*, for people are too wasted and frail to put up a good fight. Just a minute ago, I survived a punch by a man who made a fist but could not use it, for he was too weak for it, and thought better of it and spared his energy for better enemies. One can barely tell friend from foe in this land of walking dead. But it's not these melees that terrify me; it's the prospect of dying vainly in the chaos of waiting, for whenever bad tidings reach the waiting crowd, and people start to disperse, th possibility of a stampede looms, and death opens its jaws, and birds of prey start circling overhead, and before we know it, things fall apart, and the sky falls down.

This downtrodden place now threatens to become a lawless jungle where peace never takes hold. Already, I hear people speak with cynical contempt of the moral order. And who can blame them? These tortured souls can revert to cannibalism and remain blameless. It's not far-fetched. If this famine persists, we will soon devolve into a nation of jackals. And jackals, I hardly need to remind you, will eat almost anything, human flesh included, raw or decomposing. They would eat their own carcass if they could. But no nation can survive on its own flesh. That nation would sooner become fodder for the jackals of these desolate deserts.

I can see the insatiable beasts gathering, for they like to hunt in packs. I can picture them, vying for our flesh, bones, and blood. My skeletal frame trembles as I recall the sight of that poor dead child dangling from the wild dog's mouth—musing, in my shattered imagination, that soon enough I could be hanging lifeless from a wild hound's gory teeth, like sure prey, inconsolable by the prospect of providing a blessed feast of rotten human meat to a starving beast! I already look like a corpse; easy prey, ridden with fear, which the jackals can surely smell if they draw closer. Nothing gives you away to the wild dogs like fear. I learned that truth the hard way.

I was always afraid of dogs, and they could always sense it, smell my primitive fear of the species. When I was a child, a mad hound unshackled itself suddenly from its owner and leaped at me, and I fell to the ground and battled the wild beast with my bare hands and feet. But he plowed on, and leaped at me with renewed ferocity, howling fiercely, madness in his eyes, his drooling maw splitting wide to reveal his blade-like teeth. On he leaped and bit firmly my hand, and would not let go before he got a piece of me as a souvenir, where an old scar now sits. I feel sorry for the wild dogs of these quarters, who can no longer bite or howl, hardly moan, let alone bark. They walk among us like corpses, like shells of their former wildness, and they can't understand why.

The suspension of flour has reaped its first victims in the camp. It has hit the little ones the hardest. A boy, aged ten, had been wasting away and dying of hunger for days, lying motionless on a small bed that kept expanding under his frightfully dwindling body, sunken cheeks, bare bones, and hollowed eyes. For days, his parents sat helplessly by his bed and watched him fade away. His father shared an older photo of the boy in his better days, looking healthy and happy, and full of life, with plenty of meat to burn! He succumbed to starvation this morning, dying in his weeping mother's arms. He weighed ten pounds when he died. It was frightful to watch, a chilling sight to those unfamiliar with true horrors. His death has sent shocks of terror through the devastated camps. Falling like broken prayer beads, five other children have died of hunger since dawn, and many more will likely die if this horror continues.

Many a newborn could die in the cradle, as baby milk has been depleted, and mothers' breasts have dried up, and the last cows perished from hunger. I hang there trying to picture, in my debilitated mind, what it means to die in the cradle, to die upon arrival, before you even learn your name—what goes into a newborn's head as he contemplates his inexplicable fate. It's quite surreal, if you think about it. I can hear the poor thing scream with irony: "You conceived me, held me in dark suspense for nine long months, cut my umbilical cord and untethered me from the cozy comforts of the womb, and brought me into this world to *starve* me?" Surely he was safer in the womb; if he suffered there, we could not see it.

People are denied the dignity of grieving. You see a mother, holding two children in either hand, one dead, one alive. She dashes about in hysterical panic, screaming, undecided whether to mourn the dead or help the living to safety. Perhaps she can feed the one and pat and lament the other, while dodging madness with her feet.

In the middle of the stream, a mother stands consoling a starving boy withering away like a dry palm branch, his weeping fading into a faint whimper. She then retreats through the crowd and vanishes for a while, then returns and resumes her place in the queue, looking visibly anguished. You notice that the child is gone, and you stand there wondering what's left for her to survive, now that her child is dead? But it's human nature; we survive because we follow our instinct. Humans are born defiant, and they would cling to life even when life itself ceases to exist. Or perhaps this eerie clinging to survival is nothing but a distraction from all that greater loss. Perhaps this flour queue is merely a ruse to lend purpose to our shattered lives. Perhaps we are simply mad and blind to it. Perhaps in our mad rush for survival, we have become deaf to the wails within.

Standing in a sea of dying people, I scan this mass of humanity, convulsing. A dying little girl lies on the roadside wasting away, her face spectral pale, her body a mere bag of bones, while her mother sits by her side weeping, pleading with the rescuers, who look too thin and powerless to save themselves. She sits there showing passersby a photo of her child in her better days, looking healthy and happy—a joyful snap from her recent birthday, which could be her last.

Those who survive fare hardly better, and the farther the flour rumor travels, the more victims it reaps. A boy has walked for miles from a remote camp to fetch flour for his family, only to collapse from exhaustion upon arrival. You should've seen him, lying lifeless on the ground, dreaming of the flour that never was. He reminds me of the ancient soldier who ran for miles and miles to his hometown to break the happy tidings of a victory, before dropping dead at the gate. Now a whole nation can drop dead at the gate, and no one will sing their song. It will be very quiet here, except for the birds.

Any surge of hope has been trammeled by this suspension of aid. There is nothing in our power to hasten it. All we can do is wait, and wait. We are besieged by land, air, and sea. The gates are tightly sealed on our side, and the borders firmly walled. Aid ships sailing our way have been bombed at sea, burned and drowned before reaching our shores, sunk deep with those who sailed them. The heavens pour down nothing but bombs and destruction, and the scorched earth yields nothing but death and desolation. On occasion, leaflets drop from the sky, asking people to surrender, though no one is fighting or bearing arms. Kids repurpose those as toilet paper or sheets to cover the dead. Airdrops have proven deadly and killed more people than hunger ever did, for every time they drop food that way, it so happens that the parachutes fail to open and freefall on people's heads. Surely, it's not the manna from heaven you read about in the sacred books. Why not open the gates and let the trucks in? It seems the sane thing to do, if sanity ever existed on this earth!

People have taken to praying of late. It helps them cope, even when the heavens seem to fall silent. They pray in total submission, seeking refuge in a place on the verge of annihilation, feeding their empty bellies on lavish spiritual fares. With the last shred of power left in them, they stand uplifted and pray to heaven. For all the unspeakable misery they have witnessed here, people still have faith in heaven, if only as a last resort, for they would go mad if they believed otherwise. With bleeding wounds, bleeding hearts, and grieving eyes, they pray, weep, and quietly cope with their loss. They all pray to heaven, as all earthly pleas have fallen on deaf ears.

You must understand that we pray to heaven so much not because we are fanatic or deluded, but because we have no allies on this Earth. We feel abandoned and forsaken, and are languishing under siege. I always prayed as a child. I feared God; I truly did. I dreamed of heaven and all the flowing rivers of milk that awaited me up there if I followed the right path. And yes, I was afraid of hell. Who isn't? I was told that hell had a depth of a seventy-year journey, and that scared the hell out of me. Little knowing that hell was awaiting us here, on this earth, burning with a thousand fires. My father, praise be, was a tireless prayer. He had a permanent bump on his forehead, a token of lifetime devotion. He had swollen toes from constant prostration and constant displacement. He prayed in a state of total submission, bowing, kneeling, rising, as if unsure about the best way to please his Creator. And he feared for me. He wanted to save my soul. Bless his soul! He feared for my soul and the shame I would heap on him if I died in sin and went to hell. And who can blame a father for wanting to save his son from the eternal flames? Imagine my righteous father luxuriating in heaven while his son burns underneath! But he also believed in eternal justice and everlasting happiness, for which the oppressed were bound, having suffered greatly on Earth. Or so he believed. I remember those days as I weep from exhaustion, while coping with a sudden and irresistible desire to pray.

I'm starting to come to terms with the sad conclusion that I will soon die of hunger, starved to death, in this glamorous age of shared humanity. I never imagined that I would die this way, not in *this* century. I thought the age of sieges and forced starvation was long gone, folded for good. In my happy innocence, I thought the era of great famines had come to its miserable end. I thought the last victims of famine, our unlucky ancestors, were smiling down on us from heaven, hailing our age of human progress with eternal salutes!

But I was wrong. Humans will always find modern ways to justify old crimes. There will always be wars, and more wars, and still other wars. In the name of civilization. In the name of peace and justice. There will always be wars waged in the private interest of grandiose leaders and superior nations, sometimes to crush a weaker nation, but never for a noble purpose, for such a war never existed in human history. When once asked what he thought of human civilization, my father quipped, invoking a wise man, that it would be a very noble idea.

Once upon a time, the old people of this Earth knew little beyond fetching fresh fuel for the fires. Now, the new people can burn enough fuel to whirl themselves around the globe, on the way to bomb the old people. It's always been that way. Except that today it's done with flair and panache, and patriotic melodrama. They would starve a whole nation, celebrate it, and find no one among them to condemn it. Gone are the days when a prisoners' hunger strike would cause a global shudder! I picture those world leaders, so-called, convening in glitzy hotel galas and grand conference rooms to discuss our tragedy, enjoying their convivial cocktail parties, beating on their chests and patting each other on the shoulder, regaling themselves with medals and decorating one another for outstanding bravery, boasting and saluting themselves on the good and honest work of philanthropy, while the real subjects of history starve to death behind walls. They say those philanthropists are so sensitive to world disasters they can put together a charity ball within hours of a human calamity. Somewhere in the world, in a seaside resort, or a mountaintop retreat, they would meet with excited urgency and drone on about global poverty and peace, and yet never tell you that charity was invented by superior nations to perpetuate poverty and suffering on this Earth, to entertain their retired generals and warlords, who will proceed to send their hearty hails to the oppressed and wretched of the Earth. They look down on the oppressed with lofty contempt as if they were animals, believing that when they spit on their victims, they should receive it as a baptism. They plunder and loot, and steal from smaller nations with great ships, and hail their piracy a great conquest. For if you steal with a flimsy little boat, you are a thief, but if you plunder with a colossal ship, you are a conqueror. It's always that way. They prey on the weak like wolves, and when at long last they luck out and die, they get washed pure in the blood of lambs. They build glittering towers on the ruins of the uprooted and call it civilization. They hail war as peace, and declare peace only when the victims are too ravaged to bother with.

I remember my mother in those days, reading *War and Peace*, living the one, dreaming of the other. She liked to read when she could afford it. It was a good time to read, with books abounded in plenty. Sadly, books that survived the bombing have been repurposed to cover the faces of the dead, but that's another story, for another book. One day, we went out to sea, and she sat there on the sunbeaten sand, bathing in bright sunshine. She seemed engrossed in her colossal book, as if savoring a moment of spiritual escape in a land under siege, perhaps dreaming of the freedom she never had. When my young brother braved the mighty waves that day, having ventured far out, and drowned in the deep blue sea, I broke the bad tidings to her, and witnessed the first stirrings of horror on her beautiful face, a blank terror no words can express. There she sat beside his lifeless body, weeping and stroking his hair, her face white as a corpse, her eyes bleeding colorless pain. My young brother drowned chasing a fish, not for sport or pastime, but because he was hungry. Never trust the calm sea! It sets you up, lures you in, and sucks you down.

It's not uncommon in these quarters to die chasing food. I remember the Doves Well of the seaside mountain; an ancient stone well that echoed far and deep. It was dug by nature so deep into the ground that it took a stone a full minute to reach the bottom. A boy drowned there once. He was chasing a dove around the edge before he slid down and fell to his final demise. The boy was hungry, and in his starved mind, he dreamed up a dinner plan to catch the dove for his mother to stuff with rice and nuts. How fancy! The camp summoned a diver to pull him out. It was a warning tale, which our wisemen repeated with tireless passion to keep us away from the well. But we returned, and returned, until one day a military truck charged in, and poured cement into the well. It was a sad sight to see our beloved well gone in ruins, buried in its waters. Even the native doves and pigeons that once graced this land and roamed our free skies have vanished. I remember them, gathering in flocks on the grounds and brawling over crumbs of bread, which once abounded in these quarters.

My sad reveries come to a happy halt when the girl with the freckled face and oval eyes drops her bowl in exacerbation, and I pick it up and hand it to her, and our hands touch briefly. My heart pounds violently in my chest, and for a fleeting moment, I forget about my hunger, and a novel craving takes hold! But for the relentless bombing, my heartbeats would have given me away. She could sense it, my fellow orphan, and feel it, and even manage a sickly smile. It so happens that the feeblest creatures out there might give you a reason to live, like weak spring sunshine breathing new life into a long and dark winter. This autumnal metaphor becomes even more poignant if you consider her sunny smile and the red flower she's wearing in her hair, which I have noticed just now. One can still see beauty in the colorful decay of the autumn leaves.

Death looms, and life is draining out of us at a terrifying speed. Hunger rumbles on the surface and loudly below it. But our screams fall on deaf ears. The death of ordinary people leaves no trace in the annals of history. To the rest of the world, our last howls are but a fart in a hurricane—a mere nuisance. Our death rarely makes the papers, and even when our wholesome starvation finally makes the news, it's told only in the passive tense, like an act of God or some natural disaster.

But this is not what nature intended. For all its temperament, volatility, and fluctuations, nature has proven kinder to us than fellow humans. There is no denying that most disasters on this Earth are manmade, and even when nature sometimes goes berserk and acts madly, we suspect human action behind the madness, some original sin, or malicious folly—human evil to the utmost gravity. Nature has a purpose, laws, and reason. It might even possess a conscience. But what purpose do humans have? What laws rule humans, besides those of the jungle, where only the wicked tend to prevail? For thousands of years, they have fought among themselves, forming into packs, tribes, and nations, living in colossal cages they hail as states, with manned borders and high walls and gates on either side, each happily confined to its cage in the grand human zoo. Sure, they would venture out for great conquests sometimes, build colonies overseas, expand beyond the sacred borders, but they never lose sight of the cage. Now and then, they would manage to conquer another tribe, a weaker one, and create a new cage, a smaller one, seal it from the outside with manned borders and mined fences, high walls and gates, throw a siege over it, shut it by land, air, and sea, and starve those within, in the name of civilization! That's our story in tragic miniature.

It amazes me that I can still marshal these complex thoughts on an empty stomach. It appears to me that hunger is not a wholesome desolation after all, for while it wrecks your body, it gives wings to your imagination. There's music in everything, even death, for if you lend your ears and listen closely, you can hear our suppressed howls in colorful detail, and very vividly so.

I tremble in my shrinking frame as the renewed bombing shocks me out of my reveries, and all that solid philosophical reasoning melts into thin air. And imagine our horror when we discover, to our collective dismay, that the last bombing has aimed its wrath at the flour convoy!

Rumor has it that our besiegers, keen on starving us to death, have formed in packs and blocked the lorries with their own bodies just as the mystified drivers reached the gates. Another buzz has it that the lorries have been ambushed by enemy soldiers. It's impossible to reconcile these rumors, but there's little doubt that no flour is in sight. All we can see, from our grim perspective, is a fog of heavy horizon engulfed in the smoke of war, and rainbowed by the looming specter of death.

All *I* can see is that freckled face, with oval eyes, and strong features. There she stands in the haze, waiting with her empty bowl, smiling still. I suspect she's deaf, for who smiles in this hell? It's a blessing to be deaf when the whole universe—earth, sky, and sea—seems to be clamoring for your blood and conspiring against you. She is holding a fisherman's bowl, so I assume her father was a fisherman in his better days, and a handsome one for sure, she being her father's daughter, as we say. Perhaps he died in the first bombing, which targeted the old harbor with chilling precision. His tiny boat was likely bombed, burned down, and drowned in its water. O sea, source of life and death, home of the displaced! O sea, site of memories and desires, broken dreams and promises! Keeper of all flames!

Our sea was generous once, yielding more fish than we could eat. Come the war, the sea was bombed and dyed in red, and the harbor abandoned to its shores. They say when wars flare up, and humans embark on wanton bloodshed, they start with the coast, for the water makes it easy to cleanse the blood and hide the crime. The sea was our life, and now it's dead. What a farce! Even the river was murdered in its bed. For years, our poor fishermen sat by the waves and waited for peace, which never came. You could see the old tiny fishing boats standing moored to the harbor wall, tilting idly on the surf like ghosts, echoing only to the winds. I remember with awe those proud fishermen of yesteryear, with their bucket hats and long mustaches, wearing baggy trousers and headscarves lined with nets and waves, laughing from the belly at the merest provocation. I always dreamed of being a fisherman. One day, I boarded a ship, and the captain said, "Clean up the hull and follow me." I had no idea what the hull was, so I cleaned every spot on the ship, except the hull. We all laughed at it afterward, from the belly.

I loved the sea, my childhood haunt, the site of my first memories, my people's cradle and brother's tomb. I remember a boy in the heedless lap of happiness, braving the waves, building castles in the sand. My favorite game was called marbles: We drew a circle on the ground, and knocked the marbles into it—a metaphor for life under siege. A lost homeland is like a sandcastle swallowed up by the waves, slowly at first, then rapidly. I loved the sea. I loved it, calm or stormy. I liked its roar, the sound of a thousand waters. I liked the sound of broken waves. You feel the waves want to break through, but they are constantly arrested by the breakwaters—another metaphor for our siege. I smile at the day my father wanted to teach me how to swim like a fish in the Mediterranean, and I ventured too far out and came close to drowning, before a wave returned me to the shore safety.

The memory of those days gives me thrills, for even as I starve, I still recall with a smile the day I unmoored a boat in the old harbor and let it sail me whenever it may, and would proceed to revel in my aimless wandering until I was discovered and brought to safe shores. Perhaps when this nightmare ends, we could build a boat and sail together to a kinder place, and cast our old lives into the sea. Yes, I'm speaking of the girl with the freckled face, oval eyes, and strong features.

Sometimes, in my sad hallucination, I see myself in a vast wheat field, chasing my childhood sweetheart through the golden lanes. Stranded in a sea of starved and wounded children screaming in pain, I smile at the memory of two little souls chasing the cotton candy cart, barefoot in the dust, looking utterly happy. Those were happier times, heedless and free, spent in carefree loafing, upended only by war. I reminisce about the vanished landscapes of childhood, our paradise lost. I see a child, roaming freely through the ancestral citrus fields, laned with ripe oranges whose pleasant fragrance traveled between camps. Or the red strawberry fields sprawling over the green landscape, basking in the summer sun, resembling an impressionist painting. A gaunt little scarecrow draped in threadbare clothes stood there to scare the birds away. I yearn for the sacred figs, and the aphrodisiac almonds, and the bright grapes whose sweet nectar was promised to the faithful! The sweet cherries, ripening up in the summer sun, wearing the color of blood. Our pomelo tree, where I swung as a kid. The prickly pear tree, with its sunbeaten orange fruits, where I fell once and bled too freely. The beautiful loquats, and sweet jujubes, and thorny pears, those devil's tongues that can sustain thirst for days without ever whining. And the sunflowers, of course, which resembled the sun in its full glory. The aromatic guavas, yellowing in the sun. The grapefruits, changing from green to yellow, bleeding when sliced. The blood-red oranges, and mandarins, and clementines, falling underfoot, as if pleading with us to pick them.

And lest I appear biased toward the fruits, let me say that I do miss the bloody beets, red radishes, pink turnips, purple cabbages, and layered artichokes. I miss the soil that hatched them, and the earth that yielded them. I remember the harvest season and the fresh scent of the soil after the first rain. Nothing rivals the sight of olive trees washed after the first rain, with rows and rows of dark green beauties adorning the valleys and hilltops like emeralds.

A special salute to the spooky eggplants, which we fancied were inhabited by djinns. And the sun-drenched tomatoes, which flourished in these quarters. My first gastronomic memory is a colossal bowl of tomato jam that could feed a nation. The women of the camp made it while singing. It was a bloody-red festival.

I travel back in time to revisit the impressive greenhouses of my childhood, which are no more. Those sun-baked houses, lined with fragrant cucumbers and tomatoes, and bell peppers of all colors, were my secret paradise on this earth that was diminishing daily under our feet. That's where I played my first hide and seek, stole my first kiss, and sowed my first seeds. I remember my old uncle, spraying the evergreen bushes while wearing his war mask, resembling an astronaut or a space alien. It was in his lap I had my first tractor drive. I sat there and steered the machine deftly through the winding road, the seashore winds beating against my tender face. I smile at the memory of his crimson rage when he dropped his war mask between the tractor's speeding wheels, and they flattened it to the ground.

With all due respect to the modern tractor, let me raise one last salute to the horses, the oxen, and the donkeys, which have tilled these fertile soils for generations, plowing and harrowing season after season without a single whine. The tractor was a newcomer in those days, but it was no match for the mule, especially when the terrain proved too hostile for the modern machine. A plough drawn by two mules yoked together was pleasant to behold and performed magic. I mainly admired the sight of the land after a fresh plough, as if stylishly combed.

I submerge myself in nostalgic thoughts of my childhood house, which now lies in rubble, standing on its own ruins. It was old and humble, but it was home. I remember the marbled doorsteps, where I crawled as a child. The old stone front, wreathed in splendid grapevines, tinged with fallen pomegranates the color of blood, dappled with an arabesque of native trees, like living relics from a prewar past. I miss the sight of those pomegranates, falling to the floor as from Eden, the red juice trickling out of them and tarnishing the ground, resembling a crime scene. I miss the sun-colored apricots, and fuzzy peaches, and bloody plums! And the watermelons, of course, whose beautiful colors, when sliced open, make the colors of our flag, while the seeds embody our indestructible roots. The sheer memory of those watermelons, ripened to perfection by the hot summer sun, makes my mouth water.

But I also remember the red spaces that are drenched with the blood of my war-torn people, and dripping still, as if reeling from a tomato war.

Starvation looms, on the surface, and surely below it, where many people remain stranded under rubble, dead or alive, with no hope of rescue, and where an old man is laboring to dig out his family with a cane. Children are fainting from hunger in the streets. You see them rummage for food in garbage piles, while parents hang back helplessly, watching them with agony and despair, for nothing they could do would assuage the flaming fire inside the little ones. You see a father, desperately trying to fetch food from a garbage pile nearby. The pile has nothing decent to offer him, save for a bag of rotten potatoes, which he gladly accepts. You can feel the rot flying into your nose and filling it with a sour presence. Even animal food, which is hardly fit for human consumption, has been depleted. You hear of bone-thin children eating animal fodder, vomiting it, and then dying. It's not uncommon to see a child puking his guts out while worms come out of his body. Because the animal feed we have in these quarters is a far cry from the fabled pet diet that people in urban places pamper their dogs and cats with. Our animals eat fodder and hay, and other animal parts, though our women rarely discard any meat, and would cook a goat from head to toe, tripes and intestines, insides and tentacles, down to bones and blood. The hair they stuff into perfect pillows, and from which they also weave prayer mats. The blood they deploy to cleanse the old pots. Nothing kindles the imagination like poverty, and our people are as poor and wanting as church mice, and imaginative as hell.

I resist a sudden urge to vomit. I feel a rot in my soul. I fancy the worms of the earth jockeying for my body. I feel more dead than alive. There never was much hope for me. Perhaps I was born dead, and all of this is a prenatal nightmare.

Sometimes, when I plumb the depths of despair, I feel like retreating to my mother's womb, to that cozy little place without memory or pain. If I suffer there, if I starve, I will probably be too oblivious and distracted to feel it, or remember it. Mother told me once that she starved while bearing me, and I remember nothing of it. I was born in the war, and I will probably die in it. All the same. I had been dead for billions and billions of years before I was born, and I don't remember suffering the slightest pain from it. In fact, I was better dead than alive.

Hunger is the most agonizing torture. No greater pain can be imagined. It burns inside you like fire, and eats at your body. It kills you slowly but surely. They say people would eat anything when starved, but what would they eat when nothing is left, when all that's edible has been depleted and sucked dry? Dogs and cats have lucked out and perished. The few that remain look frightfully thin, roaming the ravaged landscape like walking skeletons. They will eat anything they can bite, and ask for more if they survive. Even horses and donkeys are famished. It's heartbreaking to see the donkeys, those most patient and enduring beasts, perish that way. Or the mighty horses, the most loyal of all species. Legend says that my grandfather had a horse, a very loyal horse, and when the old man died, the poor stallion stood by his grave and refused to go, until it died and perished next to its knight. His grave had no headstone, and so, for years, we would identify it from the dead horse's bones.

Nothing that moves or breathes or gives life is left standing. The place, once a sprawling garden, has been burned down to the last tree, and the last plant, and the last wheat field, and the last grain mill. The ancient flour mills, handed down from the ancestors, are spinning empty on their old stones. The olive stone pressers and the grindstones that once spun tirelessly and delighted the hearts of many children, with the vigor and tempo of life itself, have fallen silent.

Even the sea, our source of life and death, has betrayed us and yielded nothing. The relentless bombing has scared the fish away, and left nothing but rocks and sand, and dark spume. The sea turtles no longer come ashore to breed. Even the fishing boats in the nearby port were burned and sunk in their waters. I smile at the memory of the old fisherman who taught me how to row my boat, beat the winds, and cast my nets into the deep. We caught a big fish once and burst out in triumphant cheers. The swells were heavy; it took us two hours to reel in the fish. But we reeled it in, and gobbled it down. But that's all memory now, a paradise lost. Last seen, the red mullets, red herrings, anchovies, sardines, and catfish were taking flight to safer shores, never to return. One is more likely to haul in a perfect pair of shoes than fish. There is an ocean not many feet away, and we are here starving to death!

Rumors of cannibalism travel like fire through the camps, before being shortly dispelled as more people choose to die of hunger than eat human flesh. We are not mad with martyrdom, but our human dignity forbids it. We would sooner eat garbage than eat one of our own's flesh. I'm not loathe to be among garbage, our dirt, for I came from it. I was a kid infatuated with the dump, my secret playground, where I spent endless hours playing, rummaging, hunting for treasures, which never turned up. I remember a kid, newly orphaned, who survived hunger by crashing funeral feasts and scavenging leftovers at weddings, who boxed and wrestled his way into food lines and rummaged in middens for toys. My best toys I crafted from fallen rocket parts and unexploded bombs. Holes and craters created by bombs were my swimming pools, playgrounds, and hiding places. My favorite hangout was a wrecked airplane, a war leftover, which lay abandoned on the roadside like a permanent landmark. I remember my childhood pals, serving pretend airplane meals, playing war and peace, flying over the world. We never did truly fly, born under siege and all, except on those magic carpets spun in our childish imagination. Our skies are a permanent warzone, the earth is on constant fire, there is nowhere to fly or land. I always dreamed of flying free, wearing giant wings and flinging myself into the air, whirling my birdlike body through the sky, flying over the border walls, traversing hostile deserts, mountains, and seas. I smile with a pained reluctance at the memory of my flying adventure, when I attached wings to my person and flew over a cliff at a considerable distance, before I nosedived and broke my tender bones. Innocent dreams! The sky is falling, and the earth is shrinking rapidly under our feet, and there is nowhere to fly except down into the abyss. Death is looming.

As I fight my way through the crowd, I recognize a young man, dwindled beyond recognition, save for his neatly combed hair that immediately gives him away. He's an old pal of mine. He was quite an eater in his better days. We nicknamed him *vacuum,* which he was. He ate twice as much as we did, then stole our food, gorged it down, and asked for more. He ate twice and suffered twice more when food became scarce. People say that in the last war, he went so hungry he opened an abandoned vacuum cleaner to look for food crumbs inside. He shared a desk with that boy, Sugar Cane, thus nicknamed because he was so skinny yet would suck you dry if he went hungry. He had a pair of exceptionally long ears. He was a legendary eater too, though it never showed on him, except perhaps his ears, which kept growing. A yellow grin crosses my face as I hang there eyeing the young man in the slight frame. I bit him once, for I had sharp teeth then, which I freely deployed in fighting, and he was so fleshy in those days he made for easy prey. Like a little zombie, I stuck my bloody teeth in his arm and pressed on. He squealed and screamed like a mouse as I bit firmly on his arm. I did not stop until blood oozed out of it. It took a brigade of strong kids to pull us apart. I was quite a biter then, a shark among humans. It all ended one day when I was in my uncle's arms, dangling and nestling, and growing restless, I bit him firmly in the nose, and it bled freely. Shortly after, I had my teeth trimmed.

A bout of irresistible craving overtakes me as I stand there brooding over those lost times. A feeling of delirious torment, born of extreme and prolonged hunger, gives rise to momentary hankering for the most forbidden meal, like a wild beast salivating for its own kind. But I resist the image, and stifle it, and feed my heart with the thought that death is not the worst of destinies, and may indeed prove kinder to me than this life.

You know starvation is devouring your people when garbage trucks cease operating and stand idling by the side of the road, deserted like warplanes in peacetime, save for a group of starving children rummaging in vain through the empty containers. In those days of plenty and childish innocence, we fancied the garbage trucks were moving supermarkets, and we pursued them in earnest through the streets. I remember a child, a very innocent child, chasing the garbage truck for the sheer fun of it. One day, the driver halted, left the engine running, and offered me a ride. It was a hell of a ride, worth a thousand rollercoasters. Peaceful times!

The old dump at the mouth of the valley is no longer traceable, except as the site of a newly unearthed mass grave. Even the wild animals have deserted it. Have you seen an animal skeleton walking? I have, and it's not a pretty sight. Dogs, cats, donkeys, and horses have been reduced to bare bones. The poor dogs resemble walking corpses. Are they too weak to eat us alive, or perhaps they act out of canine loyalty to the people? It's hard to tell, but whatever you think of the species and their motives, they seem more humane than they let on. We have a pact with the animals. It's not uncommon in these quarters to hear a little child pleading with her cat not to eat her after she dies. Perhaps the poor kids have witnessed this horror, and they fear a similar fate. It's truly a dystopian sort of magic realism that's more magical than real.

The familiar smell of dead animals is horrendous. It's choking the very air we breathe. An army of flies is hovering over the carcass of a donkey, or perhaps a horse—a beast reduced to bare bones so that it's no longer identifiable. The flies are the only creatures that seem to fatten up rather than thin out in this human jungle. And the vultures, of course, except these scavengers are more patient, and would often wait for the carcass to rest into sun-cooked meat. And there are the hyenas, who would eat anything left by the vultures, and other nameless predators, and still ask for more if they survived.

Animal survivors hardly fare better. A mule has been dying for hours—a stubborn beast, even in death. You can hear the poor ass writhing in pain, braying through its dying breaths, the eagles circling over it. The poor animal has suffered and endured years of hard labor, only to die a death of unspeakable agony. He reminds me of my late grandfather, who survived endless wars and countless human invasions, only to die in his bed like a pet. Even the wild animals of the zoo, the mighty lions, fierce tigers, and other wildcats we thought imperishable, have perished from hunger. And the camels, immortal ships of the desert! And the sheep—if only they could wait for the butchers! You could hear the lambs, bleating sadly, choking, dying a death of indescribable agony. You can hear the bells of impending death tolling from every corner of the Earth. You can see the little children trembling in their hollowed frames, visibly mortified by the chilling prospect of a fallen bomb, where bomb scares are always imminent, and nothing is sure but the glint of death emerging from the darkness.

The flour line dissolves, and people disperse in despair, not knowing where to go, or how they will survive, or for how long. Those who still have life in them resume their wartime chores, burying the dead, pulling victims from under the rubble, or giving up and dying from hunger and exhaustion. Others are busy saving themselves, as the bombing has not abated one bit, and it shows no signs of doing so. They never find the time to lament their loss or contemplate the scale of destruction wrought upon the place. They live and die with hardly a respite.

Sometimes I suspect that the flour convoy is nothing but a distraction from the real devastation wrought upon this place. Remember when that little girl went missing for days, and then was rumored to be stranded in a bombed car, alive and breathing, and flanked by a pile of dead bodies, which belonged to her family, and the whole camp forgot about its agonies, and prayed for her survival? It's our people's way to endure the madness by clinging to a glimmer of hope in the heart of darkness. You overlook the unfolding tragedy to look for a faint gleam of light, a dim light not so bright as to awaken you, and not so dark as to dull your hopes.

The poor children resemble walking bamboo sticks. It's incredible they have held on for so long. I have noticed that the hopscotch spot has been deserted, for the kids have no stamina left to play. It's a miracle they can still stand. Except for one child, who has been hopscotching for a while through the marked squares, heedlessly and tirelessly, and long enough to hide the fact that he has a missing leg.

Parents take weeping breaks. They would stand in an empty corner over the rubble, and weep for long unbroken minutes. When they return, they resume their façades of strength and put on brave faces before the children. They were once revered as godlike and unbreakable, and still pretend to be, except when unseen. If God is weeping for us as they say, it's only because he remains unseen. But the children refuse to accept defeat. On the main road, children have loaded the corpses of their loved ones on donkey carts and wagons. A boy has loaded his baby brother in a wheelbarrow, which he shoves with great effort through the mud, across hostile terrains, under heavy rain, and relentless bombardment. Another is laboring to pull his father from the rubble, where their house once stood, before his bone-thin body betrays him, gives out, and he collapses in tears to the ground. You hear a scream, followed by a crushing sound and the rumble of a broken wheel; you look around and see a child, visibly exhausted, lying breathless on the ground with his barrow lying upside down beside him.

A bewildered child in a princess dress, who has barely started to walk, is straggling her way through ruins and smoke, alone and forsaken, seeming sad and dirty, and absolutely lost. No one is watching over her. There's no one to hold her, or take her hand, or comfort her. No one to take her home, for there's probably no home. You can tell from her wretched state that she is the sole survivor of her family. Fortunately, these little survivors are too young and tender to fathom their loss. You see a child, weeping alone beside his mother's body. He seems not to understand what death is. Perhaps he thinks she's sleeping. For when a stranger offers him a toy and lends a comforting hand, he stops crying.

On the main road, a little child in a muddy dress is pulling a pair of water gallons to safety, slightly bothered by the bullets overhead. Children are roaming the streets with empty plates and tearful eyes, with diminished frames and gaunt faces that would frighten those unfamiliar with their former appearances. This perhaps explains why those snipers are now shooting children who cross the road searching for food. Or perhaps they fear the children will grow up and avenge their parents. To save the children, rescuers are passing water gallons in boxes tied to a long rope, where children stand across the road and pull the box to safety. It's a deadly game, and it has killed more children than it has saved. As I stand there watching this most lethal game, pondering the futility of it all, a little boy exits a newly bombed house, carrying a backpack against his chest. Observing blood dripping profusely from his backpack, I approach him to lend a helping hand, only to discover, to my horror, that it contains the body of his little brother.

I catch a glimpse of my girl, standing alone in bewilderment, and it's at this moment that I conclude with conviction that she is deaf. Perhaps she was deafened in the bombing, which is not uncommon in these quarters. It's a blessing when you think about it. When the dust settles on this madness, I shall make it up to her. I will marry this girl, yes, and take her on one of those fabled honeymoons along the Mediterranean where everything you wish comes to you as if by magic. I will show her the promised land, a land beyond these skies, where the rainbow kisses the ocean. For there must be hope in all this despair, there must be something beyond the horizon, a light, a beacon, a herald of spring. Or perhaps I can take her on a joyride down to the dear old motherland. Perhaps I can unearth my mother's old necklace from the rubble and gift it to her as a dowry. Perhaps we can build a house near the old lake, worth all the silver it resembles. Or along the ancient river, flowing with the memories of our ancestors. Or beside the mighty sea, the site of passions and desires!

I imagine us in a kinder place, full and content, eating for the joy of it. We are flying over the promised land, first class, free at last. Lunch is served. Or maybe it's dinner. It's hard to tell on those occasions of timeless euphoria. There, I set out to show off my newly acquired dining etiquette. I might be poor, but I'm not a savage. See here, I can eat with a fork and knife, and quite effortlessly so! My ancestors ate with their hands and fingers, and here I am, dining across the skies like a king. I labored for years to dine in a modern manner. Manners matter, and etiquette is etiquette. And while other passengers react to the food like starving dogs to a bone, we sit there calmly, savoring every bite, digging gently into those gastronomic delights. With one napkin spread on the lap, and the other folded round the neck, we eat slowly, delicately, and with relish, while admiring the ambiance, of course, as if eating for pleasure alone. I offer her a spoonful of caviar, *real* caviar, and she smiles faintly and takes it in. *Too salty*, she says, a bemused grimace hanging on her face. The very image draws a smile on my jaded face, soothing my parched imagination.

Or perhaps I can hand her Mother's secret recipes. She made this rich traditional dish, which sent our palates dancing; she layered rice and meat and vegetables into a large pot, cooked it slowly on a glowing stove, and flipped the pot upside down when it was ready—what was its name? It's a national treasure for sure, and she kept its recipe secret. Her specialty was stuffed food. There was no vegetable or meat part she could not stuff, and that included ribs and intestines, which she stuffed with rice and nuts, and a dash of mysterious spices. My grandmother cooked a secret dish made wholly from grains and flour, which she hand-rolled into perfect pearls of edible delight. The delicious aroma of that rich stew made us salivate like hungry pups. She handed it down to her girls, and it's now my time to hand it to my girl. That's how tradition lives on in these quarters. Nothing bonds us together and preserves the spirit of the ancestors like food, which no longer exists in this doomed place, save as a distant memory.

My gastronomic reverie is cut short by the screams of people gathering over a body lying on the streetside in a pool of blood—a human skeleton wearing a white beard, a shriveled old face, and missing parts. People stand debating, with notable anxiety lacing their voice, whether the missing parts were claimed by a stray dog or vulture. The flesh is clearly torn in a gruesome display. But at least the face is intact. It belongs to the old man who breakfasted like a king. Or so he claimed.

I help the men load the body on a donkey wagon, which drives him to a mass grave nearby, where his remains will be buried. It's not uncommon in these sad quarters to bury human remains and call it a burial. One bereaved father was satisfied with a pair of tiny shoes that belonged to his little girl. It's sad to end up this way, but there's no time for mourning. Mourning is a peacetime luxury. We bury our dead in haste, to stash them away from the hovering vultures. A tiny pair of shoes is all that's left! People wish to be remembered, to leave a decent vestige of themselves. It's human, all too human. They wish to say a proper goodbye, to die with dignity, to have a visiting place, a last address that survivors can visit and where they can lament their absence. But these peacetime luxuries are a memory now. It's a sacred rite here to bury the dead. We hear some remote people burn the body of a loved one and scatter the ashes in the sea. Many of us have suffered this fate, reduced to ashes and dust, except it was done by the bombs, not a priest. We barely have jars left to fill our water. I wonder what will become of me when I'm gone. I wish to be buried near my parents and brothers, ready to embark together on our journey to heaven, though it's far-fetched, for cemeteries have filled up with the dead. One is lucky to find a coffin and a decent hole in the ground. There are no caskets, no pallbearers, and no gravediggers. Our camp had a green casket that the dead had to share. It was nailed together before the war and served the departed well. But that was when life was precious and death rare. Perhaps my body parts will be put to good use in this great cohort of amputees. I might be blind with exhaustion, but I'm not deaf to the misery unfolding around me. I can see them all—the brave children carrying on with their imperfect and incomplete bodies, yet refusing to accept their doom or surrender to despair. The girl who has lost her eye to a bomb, yet seems happy she has the other one left. She stands calmly in the line, staring at the world through her good eye, half-smiling, but full of gratitude. The boy holding his pot in his good hand, waiting defiantly, undaunted by his loss. The one-legged boy who's still hopscotching on his surviving leg, heedless of the tragedy that has befallen him.

Nothing endears life to us like death, and I have been lucky to witness so many. My most vivid memories feature funerals of fallen martyrs. They were my daily rite, my pastime. I saw a good many dead faces; colorless, featureless, sad, gone, some smiling still. I knew for whom the bell tolled, and I learned by heart what the lifeless headstones said; the names and dates and hours, the lives that had suddenly frozen in time. I heard the elegies, the howls, the lamentations, the ululations. I remember it all in awful detail. The sealed eyes, the faint odor rising from the earth, the fragrance of incense, and the perfumed bodies of martyrs. The loud cries of mourning, which could be heard far and wide. I remember the weddings that awaited martyrs in heaven, and the ones that ushered them into that heaven—the bathed bodies, the white shrouds, the green coffins.

But that's a memory now, for the deaths unfolding before my eyes are nothing like any I have ever seen. Now bodies are hurled into gaping holes, and stashed hurriedly underground with a heap of sand and mud, without so much as a bath, or a coffin, or a farewell, or a funeral, hardly a prayer. No death more undignified can be imagined. There are no white shrouds left. Children are buried with their clothes on, while parents struggle to keep whatever souvenirs or reminders their loved ones have left behind. You hear a father, weeping and pleading with the rescuers to leave him the clothes of his dead son before they bury him. Or a mother in the throes of madness, clinging to a dress that belongs to her slain child, still red with her blood. She puts up a good fight, to judge from the howls, but then she breaks down and lets go of the dress, for there is no shroud left for the child.

We no longer count our dead, or hold funerals for them, or write their names and dates on tombstones, for even if we wished to do so, most of the victims are unidentified, bombed beyond recognition. *Starved* beyond recognition. Now and then, you can identify a body from its clothes, or shoes, or a necklace, if it belongs to a little girl. But the rest are buried nameless, without a landmark, hardly a coffin. We hurl them in mass graves and bury them in haste, and proceed to preserve whatever life we can. We hardly have any power left to lift a shovel and dig a grave. The mass graves you see are craters, big holes in the ground created by the bombs, where mounting bodies are picked by bulldozers and buried in great haste. In past and kinder wars, those craters served as swimming pools for the children. Many are still buried under rubble, dead or alive, in the ruins of their bombed homes where life thrived once, and which now threaten to be their permanent graves. You see people, living ones, survivors, walking ghostlike among the rubble, looking for crumbs of uneaten food in the fissures, mindful of those buried underneath. Now and then, they would scream at the sight of a hand protruding from under the rubble, or a skull with broken teeth resting atop the sandy churned debris, or a pile of dead bones, which once belonged to people you knew, littering the surface in frightful abundance, having decomposed. There will be plenty of corpse mines to dig out when the dust settles.

I fall into a dreamless reverie, sailing into those uncertain spaces between life and death, where reality and illusion converge on the mental horizon.

Survivors have hardly fared better. On the main road, a man is riding his horse with the body of a dead child slung over the saddle in front. He's holding the little riding corpse in one hand and the bridle in the other. He seems to be riding aimlessly, bound nowhere and everywhere. Perhaps he's looking for a safe lot to bury the body, a place with a surviving landmark he could remember and visit, should he survive. On the same road, a bike is pedaling away, beating the tattered ground with its heavy treads. From the shrinking silhouette, I can make out a little boy, likely newly orphaned. He has bundled his baby brother on the back of his bike, together with their belongings and family's remains, and headed for displacement under heavy rain and bombardment. I can hear the clatter of the bike as it falls. I remember a boy in the first blush of adulthood, pedaling his creaky bike through the cobbled streets, chasing girls coming home from school. I will have you know that I was not afraid of biking without pedaling which felt like coasting. That's how I biked daily to school, and from school. Oh, school! Have I mentioned that my school, where I penned down my first words, and unfolded my first map, and unraveled the secrets of history and the universe, and discovered love, no longer exists, having burned in the first bombing?

On the very same road, a boy and a girl, likely newly orphaned, are walking with heavy treads through the mounting rubble, carrying their baby brother in a little white bundle, looking for an empty lot to bury the little body.

Have you ever seen the moon and fancied it was a loaf of bread, or a big round cheese? That's how a starving child sees the world in his dying hallucination. The sun is but a fried egg, and the stars are none but the bittersweet star fruits that graced this place once. For while it ravages your body, hunger gives flight to your imagination. What is our flag—flying with black, white, green, and red colors—but a sweet watermelon to soothe our parched mouths? What good are flags in this lifeless monochrome? What good are flying colors in a dead land silhouetted against a colorless sky?

People are in the grip of collective hallucination, like wanderers before a desert mirage. Or mystified sleepers emerging from a cave after a long slumber, too dazed to tell a dream from reality. Have you heard the story of the poor old man who bursts into happy cheers when he finds a sack of flour, only to discover, to his utter dismay, that it's only a sack of white cement? Surely you don't expect us to rebuild our homes from the rubble on empty stomachs?

Children are dreaming of food, and suffering what they dream. Hungry kids are drawing pictures of food in the sand. Bread of all sorts, but mainly homemade flatbread, for it's soft, slightly chewy, and melts in your mouth, especially when dipped in homegrown olive oil, wine of the deprived! You see a child, ravaged by hunger, drawing a piece of meat in the sand, and—God help us—eating it! The other kids laugh briefly at him before mulling it over and following suit.

I would offer a piece of my own flesh to these children, but I have scarcely any left—I smile at my mother, chasing me with her old rug duster, vowing to eat a piece of me! My skin is drying up on its bones. My shirt has widened on me; it's a miracle it's still hanging on my person. I feel like a hanger myself, having diminished to mere bones. I'm pale and sick, stinking like rot, and sweating besides. I'm nothing but a walking skeleton, a living dead, wondering by what miracle I'm still alive. I'm a ghost, and my homeland is but a ghostland, like a dead monochrome of the life that once thrived here.

I can go no more. I have lost my bearings. I feel like a bodiless spirit drifting in a timeless haze. I'm too tired to think, and too distraught to stop thinking. But I'm also too spent and worn-out to write or pen down my sorrows. No one writes on an empty stomach, trust me. You need full guts to rip open your wounds. They say there's always suffering in writing, except for hunger, for it dulls your faculties. I can no longer reflect or ponder things. I write mainly to remind myself to stay alive. It hardly matters if you live or die in this inferno, but you follow your survival instincts. I haven't the faintest idea what I'm living for; I'm blanking on it. I remember having grand dreams, but I can no longer make them out. I can dream of nothing but a moonful of bread and a fried sun. And a sea full of flour.

Hope takes on a new life as the flour convoy resumes its merciful roars behind the gates and charges steadily in our direction. In they come, slowly but steadily, judging from the approaching rattle. There's still hope in the midst of this despair. Perhaps it's not hope, but merely a relief.

People burst out in mad cheers. They embrace, pick up their empty bowls, and stand waiting, casting hopeful glances toward the gates, like bewildered soldiers emerging from a manhole in the street, believing the war is over. From the perspective of the sea, they appear as wayworn refugees stranded on a dreamless shore, waiting for the ship that would sail them to safety. It seems as if people have suddenly forgotten about their lost lives, and lost loves, and tumbledown houses, and broken dreams, and broken promises, and concentrated their hearts on this jolly occurrence—the promise of flour.

Nothing renders people more delusional than the blinding glimmer of hope. In the happy innocence of anticipation, people indulge in hopeful chatter, speaking of the future, the chances of rain, and the prospect of peace. Dreaming of life after flour. I hear a young man, a young mummy to be precise, luxuriating in thoughts of marriage and family life! Newly orphaned, he lost his family in the first bombing, lost them to the last soul. But here he is, dreaming of his future marriage, feeding his heart on the chilling prospect of starting a family of his own. Oh, the daring audacity of hope, the shameless defiance of the human will to live and survive! People may look miserable, but they refuse to be defeated. The human spirit never ceases to amaze me. Show them a gleam of hope, shine a light on them, and they will come to life and burst with bottomless energy. Perhaps we can match him with that young woman, who stands waiting in her white bridal gown still covered in red stains, and who appears to have lost her groom not long ago. There she stands, holding her empty bowl while looking at herself in a broken mirror, a hint of bridal makeup still visible on her dusty face. Broken mirrors, and broken hearts, and broken dreams, and broken promises!

I take a side glance at my girl and imagine us in the happiness of holy union. Perhaps we could set out on a long honeymoon, nestle in one of those luxury retreats along the Mediterranean. Or perhaps we can go for a walk along the local beach near sunset, and bask in the keen eastern sun, share a cotton candy cone, or a bowl of lupine, or a pair of grilled ears of corn that tastes of the native soil. Or maybe chase down a pair of ice cones in the afternoon, to soothe our fires and lessen the oppressive heat.

Love is a strange thing, an extraordinary force. No other human emotion can distract you from the torment of hunger the way love does, and while it overwhelms your heart and torments you with a new sort of hunger, it does so in such a charmed and enchanted way as to make you revel in your own torment.

The gates creak open, and in charges a convoy—not of flour trucks, but tanks manned with soldiers carrying weapons. Our besiegers have sent in troops, *armed to the hilt*, to guard the trucks, or perhaps to witness the tragedy about to unfold. They debark, file out, and stand there in a perfect display of force, with smug faces and bloodshot eyes, and hands on the trigger, flanked on either side by people insane with hunger. They watch us closely, their eyes carrying the tense foreboding of something evil. You can see the heartless tanks, swiveling their snouts, sniffing, and ready to wreak havoc on this place.

To terrorize the crowd, the soldiers unleash a barrage of gunfire in the air. The crowd disperses in places, and some who are unfamiliar with this malice scream and dash about in terror. They cast their empty bowls on the ground and scramble for safety, while the trigger-happy soldiers stand there laughing with considerable delight. And even briefly the line holds, as some maintain astonishing calm, the terror of starvation clearly overpassing that of gunfire. Perhaps they are tired of ducking and dodging fire, and would rather die by gunfire than surrender themselves to a slow and agonizing death. Or perhaps they are seeking escape from the unending chaos.

Not satisfied with terrorizing the queuing crowd, soldiers unleash their dogs on the camp, mauling people for sport, and assaulting children where they lay. I have a crippling fear of dogs. When I was a child, a soldier let loose his dog, which lept at me, mauled me, and took a piece of me as a memento. I never truly recovered from that encounter. There I lay on the ground writhing in pain, moaning and bleeding like a wounded animal, a warm blend of human blood and canine saliva wafting into my nose, while the soldier walked away laughing, leash in hand, without so much as looking back to see if I was alive. I can still hear that laughter echoing through the years. I can hear the hounds' howl now, rumbling wildly through the ravaged camp, mad fury and vengeance in their eyes, crying for our blood, as if we had blood left in our withered veins!

Then the enthralled soldiers embark on a deadly game. They gather men in groups and parade them to a death squad. In an eerie spark of wartime humor, the soldiers offer the men a chance to race forward while the bullets whizz by; the slowest ones would die first, the fastest last. It's the same death, only seconds apart. The men brace their luck. The guns fire, and the men dart forward like terrified sheep, keen on their dear lives, scrambling for the handful of extra breaths that destiny affords them, clinging to their survival, and the common joy of staying alive, however briefly. Tickled by the sight of it all, the squad officers burst out in mad laughter—lucky for the men, they lose the focus to fire further. Then their mockery turns darker: You see soldiers take twelve men at a time, lead them at gunpoint into a bombed hospital. You hear twelve gunshots echo inside, before the soldiers return, laughing still, and take another dozen. And so on.

I brace for the inevitable end, which never does come, for the soldiers have now turned their wrath on the animals, shooting them for sport, as if they were not in death's throes already. The poor animals had done nothing to warrant this cruelty, but the banality of evil is too boundless to contemplate. The bullets whizz by in mad succession, the air punctuated by the staccato notes of a war symphony. It appears the soldiers are now shooting anything that breathes, and when they find nothing breathing, they shoot the very air we breathe. They seem more terrified than they let on, visibly incensed, screaming constantly, shooting with fury at anything moving. A fallen tree leaf would provoke an unceasing rain of bullets. These magic machines never run out of fire or tire of shooting. They are made to kill in great quantity. Even the little birds have fled, and it's doubtful they will ever return. The dogs have been acting strangely. Unleashed by these human horrors, they have chased the soldiers through the camp, howling and assaulting them. Even dogs can smell evil. Or it's fear they smell. The dogs are perhaps terrified not of the people, for dry bones can scare no one, but of the dark horrors that tether them, and which now shroud this place.

Then a miracle unfolds as a wave of honeybees breaks out of its beehives and runs riot, and instead of assaulting our people, the unhinged bees, as if divinely sent, chase and batter the soldiers with stunning determination. Even these humble insects can sense evil. You should've seen the godsent bees, humming and buzzing like the sound of a thousand drones! They say bees die after they sting—nothing more martyrish can be imagined. We all laugh when the enraged soldiers open fire at the bees. We laugh even more when our besiegers airlift an entire battalion to rescue the soldiers. The planes tried to bomb the bees, but it was a futile tactic, for the bees proved too elusive for the bombs. It's laughable how humans attempt to solve everything with bombing!

The scene has evoked distant memories of homegrown honey, sweet in the mouth, warm in the heart. I remember the beautiful honeybees going from flower to flower, collecting the sweet nectar that delighted many hearts. I see a child in the lap of happiness, chasing the winged insects among the flowers. I was never afraid of bees, for they only assailed in self-defense. I picture a boy in the early flush of boyhood, chasing birds with his sling-shot, hunting not for sport, but to feed himself and fatten up on that rococo homeland delicacy. Innocent times!

By the time the gunfire comes to its miserable conclusion, the flour line is disbanded, and the crowd largely has dispersed, like broken beads on a string.

But there are people in this land who are stubborn mules. I'm speaking of the women who have stood fast and barely flinched through the whole carnage. These women are astonishingly resilient. For all the bloodshed unfolding, they are the ones who keep the line standing. You see a mother, holding a bowl in one hand, and a child in the other, her face determined, her eyes defiant. Her hands busy, she would stand fast and fight with her body, like a bear defending her cubs. You see a girl, standing in the queue under a barrage of fire, holding firmly to her empty bowl with astonishing determination that humbles a nation of men. Starving, thirsting, soaked in sweat, chilled to the bone, out of breath, people press on because to do otherwise would mean surrender.

I tremble with disbelief at the shock of being alive, and when I look at my girl, our eyes meet for a moment too long, and on her face I see a sign of relief, as if she was excited to see me survive, which gives me thrills, for it reveals to me the first stirrings of a blossoming love in a place where nothing else blossoms. There is a sad yet furtive look in her eyes that rivals a thousand love verses. I have yet to figure out their exact color. They could be green, or olive, or olive-green. Riddled with dust but rimmed with kohl, they give the impression of sad gray. It's a new feeling to me, a novel emotion, a feeling so intense it makes you forget about death's stalkings. But it also terrifies you, for now you have a reason to survive, someone to live for, and you have no excuse for retreat or surrender. I smile at her, though judging from my deplorable state, it's doubtful my smile still shows. It's only when she smiles back that I notice for the first time the small, beautiful gap in her front teeth. They part away enough to send my heart dancing in my chest. And imagine my utter enthrallment when the heavens thunder, and a few moments later, the downpour comes at last, revealing to me her beautiful blue dress, the silhouetted outline of her rain-soaked body, throwing the sorry details of her starved frame into sharp relief. It was the first good rain in a long while. Instantly, the children forget all about their misery and wallow in the godsent rain, and wash their tired faces and bodies in pristine heavenly water. The women fill up their buckets, the girls wash their hair, and the men wash themselves for prayer. Only she stands there unperturbed, bathing quietly in the hail. She wears no jewels or ornaments, hardly a trinket. She's wearing a bracelet around her foot, with a name tag on it, perhaps to be identified if a heartless bomb shatters her beautiful face beyond recognition. It's no secret that our women go to sleep fully dressed, lest they are bombed in their dreamless sleep and discovered under rubble in an immodest state. If only my mother knew it!

It's a strange feeling to be alive when many others have perished, and stranger still when you find yourself the sole survivor of an entire family. There is the initial guilt, of course, but then a secret thrill takes hold, the thrill of being chosen by destiny to live, to tell the tale perhaps, to face and rattle posterity and tell all that happened to us here. Oh, blind destiny! You feel like a chosen one, divinely saved. Perhaps it's destiny's way to say that it's not all gloom. Or perhaps your survival is nothing but a curse, a sly arrangement designed by fate to make you witness horror in its full bloom, tell the tale, and die of grief. You feel like a doomed one, in a doomed place, and in doomed times. But there is a girl, a beautiful girl, with a freckled face and oval eyes, and strong features, who believes that your survival is not in vain, that there is a purpose, a *kismet,* a mystical logic behind your survival—that people survive for a reason, they survive to live and love again, and not to merely exist or defy death. Perhaps living and loving is our best revenge, our last spit in the face of injustice. Maybe love *is* our ultimate pursuit, and all else is just a chimera. People speak of freedom, justice, and dignity, but those things are rather abstract to me. Only love is real, to go through hell knowing that my life matters to someone—knowing that someone in this sad land, a beautiful soul, is praying for my survival. It appears to me that my love, being so intense and powerful, has made a deep impression on this destiny. I could have been shot, I could have been kidnapped and tortured to death, but somehow providence has arranged for me to stay alive. Here is a girl, a bashful young girl in the early flush of womanhood, who gives me a reason to live where nothing but the dark glint of death breathes. I have yet to learn her name, or story, or dreams, and already I feel that we are destined for each other, doomed, *condemned* to be together. We feel like each other's kismet, as we say. There we stand, a crowd apart, not a word spoken between us, yet feeling perfectly in love.

The soldiers have once again made their intentions clear. They have sown terror among the hungry, mocked us to death, and made fun out of pure cruelty.

Survivors continue to preserve whatever life remains. The flour queue is forming out back again, less tidy, but forming nonetheless, with the soldiers still on watch, as if dry bones can harm anyone. From the sheer appearance of people, one can clearly see that they have barely enough energy left to hold a bowl of flour. They are perfectly unarmed, save for a few children playing with their toy guns. Here and there, you detect a sign of normal life still beating. You can see children playing hopscotch, tag, or hide and seek. One child has been hopscotching on one leg for so long he's started to amaze me, not knowing that he has but that one leg. In a newly created wartime game, four kids are staging a funeral procession. Raising a doll on a broken stretcher, while acting like pallbearers, they march in solemn silence, lost in the act. You can hear the shouts of two survivors fighting over the custody of a clothesline—skirmishes that tantalized me once, but now are proof that there's still life in this doomed place. I can make out a woman, sweeping a toehold in her bombed home, perhaps hoping to bake a meal for her starving children when the flour comes in. You see half of the floor still hanging, while the other lies in rubble, as though life and death were jockeying for it. I remember my mother sweeping our doorsteps with her old straw broom. My father, coming home tired, shaking the dust off his clothes. My younger sister crawling, walking, growing into a young girl. My brothers fighting each other for the thrill of it. Our seaside house, crammed to the rafters with the noisy bustle of life!

Humans are a strange species, for even when you think they have hit a new nadir, they still show astonishing resolve. An old man has hired an excavator to dig out his family from the rubble and bury them properly. For days, he has labored in vain to dig them out. When night falls, he sleeps alone amid the ruins where his house once stood, then rises with the sun and resumes the search, occasionally casting his shovel into the ground in exasperation. He strikes me as a living dead, a shell of his former self, but the persistence with which he pursues his search mission can only be described as superhuman. A weaker man would dig his own grave and lie in it, and wait for the cold hand of death to strike him.

There's still life in this dead land, beating faintly but surely, for as the bombs rain down, and the flour trucks tarry, and the soldiers stand in menacing poses, and the earth goes up in flames, two old men sit under the red sky playing backgammon amid the ruins, smoking like dragons, laughing and coughing in one breath, and chatting about politics, the chances of rain, and the prospects of war and peace.

The familiar aroma of tobacco wafts freely through the air, as if the sky were not red with smoke already. This homegrown tobacco has the virtue of suppressing your appetite and craving, while blunting your taste buds—though it does make you doze off into a ghostly state of delirium.

Let the old men puff and smoke the pain away! They are not going to die from natural causes anyway. No one dies from natural causes in these quarters, for all deaths here are humanly sanctioned, because this hellscape is not an act of God, or a natural disaster, or some *force majeure*—it's human-made. My late uncle was quite a smoker, but it wasn't the smoke that ultimately killed him. He was a war photographer. He took my first photo, which features me marching along with my father, hand in hand, to stop the war. Oh, the happy delusion of peace! That photo has outlived time itself; twelve wars and still hanging! I remember him roaming his studio, watering and drying his photos, a cigarette dangling from his mouth, unflicked ash hanging precariously from the butt. He smoked like a restless dragon, rarely pausing for breath. He coughed often, incessantly, until one day the music stopped. He died in the last war. He died with the evidence; a bullet pierced his camera and rested near his heart. Nothing remains of him. Hardly a photo.

"Have a puff!" says the old man when our eyes meet. "No one's immortal, son." The other man nods in agreement. "Listen to the old man," he says. "A puff won't kill you." He tells me a strange story of a man who quits smoking to witness the liberation of the homeland, only to die in the bombing. "No one lives forever, son," he says, pausing for a cough, which lasts dreadfully long, morphing into a frightful whoop. "Except maybe war criminals!" he adds, laughing hard. He is toothless to boot, choking on his own smokes, holding his heart and beating on his chest. I fear for his life, though if he does choke to death, he would at least die content, and that's triumphant enough.

As the flour queue has morphed into a massive flood of humans, swelling at a terrifying speed, with no end in sight, a group of young men sit comfortably on a tattered sofa nearby, flanked by rubble and ruins, smoking. They have made smoking pipes from bullets, which abound here. They seem in no special hurry to survive. Or perhaps they have lost hope and set their minds to savoring a last smoke in this burning hell.

A dash of nostalgia gushes through my veins. Our old house had a green sofa that survived three generations and many wars. My father always slept on it. I remember him lying there at full stretch, finding company in the television, seeking solace and comfort in the dying of the day, avoiding his familial duties to my mother. On that old green sofa, he watched history unfold: the invasions, the inevitable exiles, the relentless wars, the fleeting victories, the lingering defeats, the false promises of peace, the bloody uprisings, the untidy killings, the unfolding loss of his homeland. He was always the one in control of the remote, believing in his happy innocence that he who held the device controlled the narrative. I remember him clinging to it like a child to his toy, utterly transfixed by the magic box as if our salvation, God's last words, the end of days, was about to unfold on that little screen. We watched the news and nothing but the news, the rolling world of events. And politics—always a thrill. That screen was our window to the world, a blind soothsayer, our oracle of hope and doom. Finally, one fateful day, our beloved bloated old sofa, the cradle of three generations, collapsed into a pile of debris. Shortly afterward, the whole country followed suit.

I have noticed that the queue has shrunk in places, owing perhaps to the fact that many people have mysteriously disappeared. It appears that people go out searching for food and never return. Perhaps they wander into one of those kill zones from which no one emerges alive. Have I told you the story of the five young men who eerily vanished while rummaging the desolate grounds for food? Five unarmed young men walking up the road are blown to bits with a bang. You wonder what invisible force has killed them so swiftly. Then you hear hysterical laughter echoing from the scene, and realize that the soldiers are having fun. For no one laughs here anymore, except the murderers. Ruthlessly, without premonition, the trigger-happy soldiers have blown the young boys to smithereens, leveling their bodies to the ground, save for a red oasis of blood, leaving hardly a remnant for their families to collect.

There is nowhere safe to go. Even the breadline here, designated as a safe zone, is now a killing field manned with soldiers and transited by heavy tanks and bulldozers, a human minefield ready to detonate and wreak havoc at the merest excuse, as if our righteous killers needed an excuse to kill.

Besieged by land, air, and sea, people have nowhere to go. All escape routes lead to certain death. The earth is a burning hellscape, the skies a hanging hell, and the sea a giant tomb. They could tunnel as they please, but they would eventually resurface with a cloud of blown-up mine. Many have perished that way. There's nothing but death at the end of the tunnel. Our camp is the last survivor in a city now gone. The whole land in flames, burned down to the last tree, we feel like we are standing at the edge of the desert.

"Flour, flour!" people cry out, pointing to the gates, and you know it's not an illusion because many people have seen it. Or perhaps they heard the promise of it in that approaching roar, and fortified sound with image. It is a new day, and one can see, in the red silhouette of dawn, the flour convoy drive its colossal wheels in the rain-soaked soil and slowly advance in our direction. Soon we shall put this day out of its misery, and people will fill their bloated bellies with bread, and all those hunger pangs will be a memory, and we will show the heavens that there are people on this Earth who can survive and live by bread alone. Perhaps I can marry that girl with the blue dress, freckled face, oval eyes, and strong features. We can unmoor a boat and sail away to a place where delicious pastries sit uneaten in bakery windows, luring in lovers. I bet you could stand there, your stomach growling louder and louder, but you do not suffer or feel pain, for you know that soon you will drown that growling monster in a sea of delight. There you sit, munching on your pie, pouring cream into your coffee, dreaming of the future, with hardly a memory of the past and its sorrows. Perhaps I will cook for her, yes. Nothing fancy, mind you. Just good food. A light omelet, maybe, rich with mint, and drenched in olive oil. And plenty of bread. Or perhaps we can go fishing, somewhere on the Mediterranean, where the gods of hunger never set foot. We can build a tree house, out of olive trees, oak, and pine, so when human madness kicks in anew, and the bombers of the sky cascade down, there will be no rubble. Surely wood will be kinder to us than rubble. Perhaps we can start a family, make children, for nothing delights the orphans more than a house full of children. But I warn you, in the next war you will find me prepared, stocked up on food, piles of it. Perhaps I will dig a secret tunnel and fill it with flour. No kids of mine shall go hungry. My father was a hoarder. He collected bits of solid wood, piles of it, for a rainy day. "To feed the fire," he liked to say. Not knowing of the hunger that was lurking, monster-like, waiting to feed on us.

In the delirium of hunger, their faces come alive, and with them the memory of our last bonding. I remember seven souls huddled together under one roof, holding hands under the relentless bombing, as if wishing to die together, waiting in fraught anticipation. That was the last time I remember us together. Seven masked faces sat sequestered in a windowless room, praying for safety, waiting for the madness to stop. It's quite remarkable that any of us survived. It took seconds for our bond to be broken forever, like beads falling from a string. It takes seconds to lose everyone, but a lifetime to fathom your loss, and you never truly heal. But you carry on, because life grinds on. You live defiantly, before you realize that you've frittered away a whole youth outrunning death and clinging to survival, rarely pausing to mourn, or reminisce, or dream. Then you hear the growls of a flour convoy, and you say to yourself that perhaps human life boils down to mere survival, and everything else is just a display—an image. Perhaps when flour pours in plentiful, and the ghosts of hunger are banished, and I fatten my heart on that homegrown bread, and become full and content, perhaps then my existential horizon will broaden some and wax more ambitious. For now, it's just survival.

The high gates creak open, rising slowly, but surely. I can faintly glimpse the approach of a single truck, which, imagine our dismay, proves to be the last! A truckful of flour for a whole nation on the brink of starvation. A speck of flour per person! Our besiegers are portioning our food to keep us on a starvation diet, to starve us into submission without killing us, or perhaps condemn us to a slow, agonizing death. It's a mockery, a tragicomic farce of cosmic proportions!

The truck crawls to a halt before the queuing crowd. A man in military fatigues emerges from the thick cloak of dust choking the camp, stands on a mound nearby, and starts reading a long list of banned goods, which could easily be summed up by sorting out the only substance allowed—flour.

People wait in fraught anticipation, clinging firmly to their bowls and pots, pressing them against their hearts as the scrambling crowd threatens to knock them down. Those without bowls have folded their dresses and *thobes* in a certain way to create fabric bowls resembling kangaroo pockets. It's an old practice handed down from the ancestors, which had proven quite valuable during the olive picking season, where olive groves abounded and graced these fertile quarters once, sprawling across the land and nestling in the quest foothills under the warm autumn sun. Others have rested their pots on their heads to briefly unburden their hands. It has always amazed me how old women in these quarters can juggle a bowlful of olives on their bare heads for miles, meandering through undulating roads and winding paths, down the valley and up the mountain, without ever pausing for balance or needing help from their hands.

I smile in my agony as I glimpse a kid in the crowd, picking his nose and licking it, picking and licking, without a hint of shame or apology. He does it with persistent resolution and desperate vehemence that would melt the heart of a stone. I feel sorry for the poor soul; no child can survive on that stuff. I jostle my way toward him and lead him quietly to the front of the line, to spare him the agony, and myself the unpleasant sight of his incessant picking.

Dawn is drawing near, and darkness is petering out, revealing a pack of vultures circling low overhead, which casts a pall over the gathering throngs. And beyond the vultures, the sea is roaring madly, like a pride of a thousand lions. The unusual presence of hawks flying at a low altitude does not bode well. And there is the owl, best fortuneteller of all, and bearer of bad tidings. Our ancestors mastered the art of owling. They unleashed their bird in the sky; if it flew north, it was a good omen, and if it flew south, a bad omen. And I have seen it, yes, for even in my delirious state, I can still tell north from south. But not all omens are divine. For what do you make of these crawling rats, dashing about in frenzy, as if trying to alert us in the most irreverent and undivine way? It's hardly a superstition when the frantic rats make those long growls that signal danger and command vigilance. Even the snakes have crawled away in fear.

The birds are chirping strangely, sounding like crickets. No, it's not a superstition. It's an instinct; birds trust their instinct to build nests, and we trust ours to read the birds. We people know our spaces well. We know the land and its secrets. The landscape is etched into our minds and hearts like a map. We know our topography like we know our bodies. We know the earth and its belly. Living underground for long stretches of time does not make us demons, only survivors. When the next asteroid hits the Earth, we will be the last to go. We are the salt of this land. We water it with our blood and grace it with martyrdom. We believe the land belongs to its martyrs, yes. If only we knew how many nations had perished that way, and how many will! For it's not enough to kill all birds in flight to wipe out the species; they must also destroy the eggs and the nests altogether, and the trees that house them.

People try to make a break for the truck, but grasping the futility, they give up and line up. The line is not straight or linear. It has its own structure and momentum, like an ant colony, or a deceptively chaotic beehive, or a crowded animal farm where the lambs seem always on the verge of stampeding, but never do. Except that lambs never fight among themselves or assault their kind. For one can tell from people's faces and shattered nerves that this line is teetering on the edge of the abyss. Perhaps the abyss is already gazing down on us, but we are too blind with hunger to see it. Hunger is the worst torture. No greater torment can be imagined. Even the earth shakes her great belly from time to time, opens her frightful mouth, and takes in thousands. But not our people, or children, who have not seen food for so long they hardly remember how to eat.

I tremble in my frame as the soldiers, like mad dogs suddenly unleashed, shove people with their rifles and batons as if ramming sheep into a barn to force them into straight lines. One feels like standing before hell's gate, except that we have never truly learned what sin we've committed to warrant this collective punishment. In the good old days, men fought men and died in the delusion of glory. Now men fight children and call it war, and go on living without a sense of shame or remorse. There is nothing noble about starving children. There is no splendor, and no glory. The sight of soldiers mocking the gaunt bodies of our children will shame the devil himself. It will dethrone Satan and humble whole kingdoms of evil.

The scene has rattled me to the bone. I can feel my blood boil and rise in my red veins, my body shaking with fury, my rage stirred to a froth, my belly a cauldron of repressed anger. And when a soldier shoves my girl with the end of his rifle, all the passion and desire I have harbored for her morphs instantly into a volcano ready to explode in the face of our tormentors. I let hunger growl quietly in my belly and steep in my fury. I picture myself as a savior, a romantic hero, a noble warrior saving his girl from the menacing soldiers. A knight in shining armor, as they say. It's hard to resist the temptations of fantastical martyrdom when nothing else remains, when everything else has fallen apart, all the hopes and dreams we have seen crumble before our eyes. I imagine myself in possession of great supernatural power, fighting mighty tanks with my bare chest and primitive homemade arms, sometimes with nothing but a slingshot and a little stone. Masked as a batman, I fire at the tanks at close range. I ambush soldiers and liquidate them with homemade dynamite. In my unbridled bravery, I have morphed into a Samsonian martyr, bringing down houses on the heads of my besiegers, who had turned the homes into rubble. Having turned our ruins into trenches, I ambush soldiers inside abandoned homes. I batter tanks and bulldozers with rocket-propelled grenades, and gun down trigger-happy soldiers as they lie basking in their victory. I'm a righteous god bringing justice to the oppressed. I *am* justice! You should've seen me, sniping that soldier! There I sit, quietly and birdlike, hiding in the ruins of our bombed home, biding my time, eyeing the monster with my cool yet deadly patience, haunting him down while crying out with disbelief—the disbelief of a powerless young man who finds himself suddenly empowered. The disbelief of an orphaned generation who rises up from the ashes to avenge their fathers. Revenge is a noble feeling indeed. It's justice, sweet edible justice. Oh, if only my girl could see it! If only my mother, father, and slain brothers and sister could see it! It would be a spectacle to watch. My only regret is not being in the crowd to see myself perform.

It appears my imaginary resistance has made quite an impression on the soldier. The monster could sense it, for as I indulge in my fantastical thoughts, our eyes meet eerily. His gaze rests squarely on me. His bloodshot eyes scan my body with menace and suspicion. Inside me, all hell breaks loose. I burst into a scarlet fury, the kind you reserve for your worst enemy. And what enemy is worse than those starving you to death and reveling in your agony? My heart rails and fumes. I feel in the grip of madness, my eyes glowing with crimson fire, blood flooding my face and rushing to my ears, my teeth set on edge, my head a ticking bomb, my thoughts violent and bellicose. A warlike fever overtakes me, wiping away every vestige of peaceful manners. It's as if all the anguish and humiliation and frustration of the past hours have boiled over. I pull out my imaginary gun and shoot him right in the face without mercy or remorse, bursting into hysterical triumphant laughter. I'd often daydream about shooting callous monsters who deserve it, right between the eyes. That's how I killed my past tormentors, and my family's killers, and all those monsters who think they can escape justice and bask in impunity. There's no place for weaklings in this world. It's a cold wilderness, and people who are powerless, who allow themselves to be powerless, have no place in it. The weak and meek and the cowards shall live and die in the shadow, like a rootless tree ignored by the sun. The people of this land invented the art of silent resistance. Resistance means a daring and direct look in the eyes, a boiling in the blood, a muted protest in the bones—a fearless look at death.

But no sooner have I declared my silent resistance than the bastard senses my fury, and orders me to step aside, and when I refuse, beats me with his rifle right on the head, and I collapse to the ground, my face soaked in hot blood, my eyes blinded from pain. It's as if a magician had thrown a blanket over my eyes, and I'm in the dark. Only she, the girl with the freckled face, oval eyes and strong features, comes to my rescue, shoving the soldier aside and sealing my wound with a fold of her blue dress before lending her small and tender hands and helping me to safety. Those hands have brought me from the depths of despair, for sometimes, when life reaches a new nadir and death becomes a sweet prospect, you summon the courage to look death straight in the eye and let him know that you are not afraid of him, that you wish him—*dare* him to strike. But this girl will have none of it, for I can feel now that she wants me to live, and what could possibly make life worth living as those loving eyes gazing down at me so kindly and casting soft light into the darkness into which I have drifted?

In the bloody hours of dawn, the truck crew unload the flour sacks. They stock them in untidy piles before the waiting crowds, where more children have been queuing up with empty pots to receive flour for their families, but mainly for themselves, as most children here have no surviving families. The scene resembles a nation in the throes of mass exodus, like chaos before creation. From the perspective of extraterrestrials looking down on us, the place resembles a black hole on the verge of explosion, except that people here are taking extraordinary human measures to prevent the scene from descending into chaos.

It's believed that human agency can follow a more predictive path than nature, even when you factor in extreme hunger and human malice. But then chaos ensues as the flour line quickly dissolves, and like a sudden flood, people start to push forward and stumble over each other, and stampede to their deaths. The gates of hell break open, like an abyss that threatens to eat us alive. It all happens when suddenly the waiting troops unleash a barrage of gunfire on the heedless crowd, and like red beads falling from a broken string, people start to fall to the ground, red blood gushing out of them. Like a cascade they fall—children, women, old men, with empty bowls and empty bellies, slaughtered in their dreamless euphoria, deprived of their last wish to eke out a bowlful of flour from the maws of hunger and destitution. Down they go, while still clinging to their empty bowls, which quickly fill up with their own blood. A river of blood flows like a stream on the ground and blends with the spilled flour, like freshly made henna paste. You should've seen the monsters, firing indiscriminately at people as they stumbled for the spilled flour, dealing them fatal blows in vital spots—in the head, chest, and stomach, as if hunger was not killing them already! You see children, dashing madly about with their bowls of flour, jockeying for the nonexistent safety, before falling to the ground and sinking into eternal sleep, their little faces wholly covered with flour, as if wearing a red-stained kafan.

As people lie lifeless on the ground, a fleet of military tanks and bulldozers charge on and crawl with heedless brutality over the bodies—dead, wounded, *alive*—turning them into minced meat for the hovering vultures, and casting a dark pink shade on the ground. No trace of them remains, save for a cloud of flour, and a tract of red soil, to which they have returned, as if reunited with the earth that birthed their ancestors—a ready fertilizer for the soil from which they came. You should've seen the heartless crawlers, ramming over the bodies with startling malice, leveling them to the ground, which now threatens to become their grave. It's hard to find a whole body. It's hard to find anything resembling a human figure. I can identify a small hand protruding from the ground. It must belong to a little girl, for its wearing a bracelet. You see a toe there, a finger here, minced meat everywhere, but little else.

What started as a breadline has now morphed into a mounting pile of bodies, hastily picked up with bulldozers and buried in waiting craters. No tombs, no funerals, no eulogies. Thanks to the bombs, the graves need not be dug. The craters lie there, waiting for the dead, like the deep abyss of hell. Yet many bodies, having eluded the crawler's teeth, remain strewn on the ground. No one ventures to collect them, as most survivors have dispersed and scrambled away in fear, making a dash for the safety that does not exist.

The scene resembles a slaughterhouse. Most victims are children, their tender little bodies in piles. I can hear a heartbroken mother screaming madly through the crowd: "My little girl is gone; she's been starving for seven days." Alas, her rather universal description solicits no response from the crowd. "She had a ponytail," she adds, though given the ubiquity of slain little girls with ponytails, I fear she needs to be more specific. It helps if the girl is wearing a crown, or a hairband, or even a flower, though it's doubtful these ornamental features can survive intact. Hair locks and clips are scattered on the surface. Shoes, sandals, jewels, and crowns that once belonged to little children. Broken toys and broken dreams. It's rare to find a full body. One is lucky to find a body part, or a few remains, though matching those scattered remains into an identifiable whole would be akin to solving a puzzle. So people settle for whatever they can find. You see a horrified father screaming madly while holding a pair of sandals that belonged to his girl. It's a sad sight; you can't bury a pair of sandals and call it a grave. The vultures are hovering overhead; rescuers would do well to shove a body part in a plastic bag, give it a name tag, and stash it in the waiting ground.

It was a cold-blooded massacre, a premeditated slaughter carried out in broad daylight, for the sun was out in its full glory. I hear people dub it the Flour Massacre—or perhaps more fittingly, the Red Flour Massacre, to account for the bloodstained flour left scattered on the ground. Even our bread is massacred, murdered before it's leavened. Yet the soldiers stand there impassively, unfazed by the crime they have committed. They could've killed us before the flour truck rolled in, to spare us this horror. But no—they waited for the flour, because the crime would not be complete without the dramatic flair of slaying people amid their hopeful euphoria, depriving them of their last meal on this Earth, rendering their blood a final sacrament.

It was cold-blooded, yes, for you can see the monsters smiling smugly in the wake of the carnage, basking in the shade of their crime. You can hear them, laughing brazenly at starving children who, following the bloodshed, are laboring desperately to separate the white flour from the bloodstained, and realizing the futility of their labor, collecting the flour as it comes.

But no crime is complete without being hailed as a victory by those who staged it. You can see the monstrous drones, the finest and latest innovation of human evil, buzzing near and hovering overhead to record the carnage from the air. Surely they find the scene bemusing, the stuff of wartime entertainment. You can hear the schadenfreude, the vicious, gloating laughs of our besiegers, cheering the prospect of cannibalism in our midst—the inescapable gloat in seeing us eat our own flesh. It's not far-fetched. Flour was our savior, and they murdered it. Even the flour truck, our vehicle to salvation, was riddled with bullets. Rescuers and aid crew were shot with chilling precision. And the donkeys, our last surviving transports! It's a miracle any of us has survived. Hunger is gawking at survivors like a monster eyeing its prey. The beast's belly is closing up on us.

And besides the gunfire, the place was hit with a massive bomb, weighing untold tons, as you can see from the mounting rubble, which moments ago was not there. The place burned like a thousand suns, blistering the camp to the last tent, and leaving the ground nothing but a frightful monochrome of red and brown, transited by horrified survivors, and families fleeing in horror, with nowhere safe to go. It has the impression of a nuclear bomb. The sight of burning people is hard to watch without sacrificing your sanity. When humans discovered the secret of fire thousands of years ago, they surely had a different purpose in mind than burning other people alive. But humanity has progressed since. It has made unimaginable leaps, for modern civilization has little qualm about burning people to ashes, *sacrificing* them in the name of civilization. But one does not have the luxury to indulge in such philosophical thoughts when his people are in flames. Perhaps when the dust settles, and the full scale of horror is revealed, historians of war will entertain humanity with these horror tales, in good time, with the temporal distance and emotional detachment humans require before summoning the moral courage necessary to confront these truths. For it takes guts to witness this human madness while it's still unfolding, and stay sane—to go about life enjoying your daily bread while knowing that somewhere on this sad Earth, in some remote cold corner in this tiny planet, human beings are being massacred in a breadline. That's at least what I gather from the screams of those bereaved, heartbroken mothers, crying out in maddened rage and despair: "Where's humanity?" Perhaps there's no humanity. Perhaps humanity is a mirage, set out amid this vast human desert. Because if humanity indeed existed, it would have shown itself by now. If God truly meant to intervene in the degeneracy of humankind, he would have done so by now.

The deeper you walk into the scene, the more horrific it becomes. I can hear a rescuer shouting: "Whose leg is this?" People try to identify their loved ones by whatever trace they can find. A shoe here, a necklace there, hair-clips everywhere. Many victims have been buried alive, crushed by bulldozers, flattened beyond recognition. There's hardly a complete body. You see a hand here, a leg there, human meat everywhere. Rescuers are collecting body parts in plastic bags. One is raising a headless boy in the air, so he may be identified by his clothes. Not far away, a young man is being identified by the shape of his teeth. You can see children's remains still hanging from the fences. Blood is weeping on the walls. A slain girl is dangling from a hook, her legs shredded into ribbons of flesh. It's a terrifying sight, more so because no one has yet ventured to unhook her. She was likely torn asunder by the blast while trying to escape.

A sea of wounded people lies on the ground, writhing in pain, moaning through dying breaths. Death can't come soon enough to them. The angel of death can't visit these grounds quickly enough. The Grim Reaper can't uncloak his cape and land his scythe fast enough. I suspect the wounded wish not to be rescued or saved. They are pleading with us to let go of them, to be spared the horror of having to witness a loss greater than themselves, for you can see the little bodies of their loved ones lying lifeless beside them. They look around with dying stares, sheer horror in their eyes, as if wondering what has taken that dark, hooded monster so long! All you could do is fetch that monster for them, which is no easy feat, for he's probably busy reaping other lives nearby. I have seen the eternal footman hold so many coats and snicker!

An army of flies is hovering over the bodies. First come the flesh flies, who like their meat freshly killed. Then the cheese flies, who like it rotten and cheesy. Wild dogs are walking among the dead, drooling with thick slobber, barking menacingly. Very soon, there will be plenty of bone meat on the ground, and there will be no scrawny dogs in these quarters. The vultures are circling overhead, like flying omens of our doom, ready to swoop down and dig in. In the red silhouette of the main road, I can make out a dog, cantering madly across the red grounds, the body of a dead child dangling from its mouth. I hang there trembling in fear, laboring in vain to shake off the horrifying prospect of meeting a similar fate. The sheer image of my own corpse hanging from a hound's teeth shakes me to the core and assails my soul. The horror! The horror!

I feel sick and nauseated. I resist a sudden urge to vomit. All that these children wanted was to fill up their empty bowls with a handful of flour, bake it into plain bread, fill their empty bellies, and little else. All they dreamed of was a last meal; instead, they have been turned into a feast for the waiting vultures.

Few have survived, if by survival you mean mere biological existence. Humanity must invent a new concept for those who survive hell on Earth by dying. You feel like a zombie, eerily arisen, wandering among the dead. But there's no time to waste on grievances. We must collect the dead and bury what can be buried. Bodies decompose faster in this heat. You can already feel the rotting stink flying in your face, like the sour stench of death. My people's blood is crying out from the ground, which for most nations is an expression. The blood will be washed away by the rain, or the Great Flood that would one day destroy humanity for good. But the dead must be buried with the dignity they deserve. People wish to have a resting place in the ground.

Rescuers rush to collect the dead and wounded, before loading them onto donkey carts, as ambulances trying to reach the scene have been bombed enroute, with callous precision. There are no hospitals left standing, hardly a shelter. Rescuers are piling bodies in untidy heaps as if they were flour sacks. On a wagon, children, still drenched in red flour, are being laid out in a neat row, placed tightly next to one another, like dead roses in a flower bed. They will likely be buried in a mass grave, a hole in the ground, a waiting crater, as cemeteries have filled up. The place teems with bereaved parents holding white coffins the size of their open palms. The coffins, where their slain children are eternally wrapped, are dotted with visible red spots—a lasting token of the evil committed here.

People are driving the carts themselves because horses and donkeys have all but perished. We have a special bond with the donkey, a sort of kinship. Those mules of the earth have served us well through the years and put up with our unending wars and suffering. This sturdiest of creatures was my first childhood ride, carrying me across the dear old homeland, roaming from the mountains to sea, wandering through the desert, traversing hostile terrain without so much as a whine or murmur. It might as well be my last ride, for my bleeding wound is too relentless to deny any longer. It's incredible that I have held on for so long. It's harrowing that I should depart this world the same way I entered it: wrapped in white cloth speckled with red spots.

And if horses and donkeys perished, imagine the fate of weaker animals. Imagine the fate of those young children, whose emaciated bodies could hardly weather a gentle wind, let alone a monsoon of gunfire raining down. What have they done to deserve such cruelty? There are no answers, only clues, wrapped in that mystery known as humanity. But let's not dwell here. Let time intervene in some measure to assuage and lend an azure tint to their story.

It all happened in a blur, and it was horrifying. People were pouring flour into their bowls. There was the inevitable jostling and jockeying, but the line was holding, and the natural order of things followed. Children were playing and singing in the vicinity, uplifted by the promise of bread. Mothers stood dancing, not from joy, but because they were carrying their newborns in bundles tied to their chests, like kangaroos, rocking them to sleep. A clown was entertaining the children with a pretend cooking show. Then the gates of hell opened, and fire burgeoned and slashed its way through the scrambling crowd. People fell down, still clinging to their bowls. Like dominoes they went down.

I remember a breadline forming in the small hours of dawn. A great tide of humanity flowed forward, like an unending exodus trail, or an antlike refugee column, or a sea of pilgrims. There was a great hullabaloo, like chaos before creation, except there was no creation, only death. There was great scrambling and stumbling. People flocked about like frightened insects, their petrified feet mimicking the sound of a thousand beehives. Men and women, boys and girls, crowding onto a sinking ark, crying out in mad staccatos, scrambling for the safety that did not exist. They dashed about in all directions. The place resembled a miniature hell glowing red. There was a little child looking for her lost earring in the midst of all that greater loss, and a forsaken baby crying from hunger while trying to thrust his big toe into his mouth. I remember feeling warm in the chest, a burning wound reeking of hot red blood. The whole place was red with the blood of my people. Then I lost my breath. I went blind. I went deaf. I went mute, which hardly mattered, for the blood screamed louder. I seemed to have suffered a morbid loss of the senses. Then I lost my footing, briefly fainted, and blacked out into the red darkness, and swooned into a dreamless nightmare. The rest was a blur.

Somehow, it feels eerily peaceful in the ruins. In my delirium, I see all the loved ones who perished from hunger and despair waiting for me in a heavenly place. It bears an eerie resemblance to the dear homeland, to judge from the lush olive trees sprawling between river and sea. I see my mother, reading her book on an ancient rock facing the sea, drifting into her sundrenched snooze. My young brother, carried ashore by friendly waves, safe and sound. My father, sprawled on his green sofa, watching the news unfold on Earth, laughing at the absurd spectacle of mortals killing each other, musing in his heavenly wisdom that if they could wait a bit longer, they would all die ultimately. My brothers, fighting for the sheer fun of it. My sister, swinging idly in her tree hammock. My grandmother, grinding wheat on her old tireless millstone. My grandfather, smoking his pipe in the shade of his fig tree, flanked by vines on either side. And there, in the dear old harbor, I see the toothless old fisherman who showed me the ropes, reeling a giant fish that could feed a whole camp, laughing from the belly.

I rise in a ghostlike state and hobble through the bodies, dead, wounded, breathing still. Hundreds of people lie dead in a sea of blood. Children, women, men, young and old, bundled newborns, some barely a few days old. They lie strewn across the place, shot in every spot imaginable: head, chest, face, neck. Some are dead, others gasping with dying breaths. You must zig and zag your way among the bodies as if walking on a battlefield. Paddling my way across the blood-drenched landscape, I feel like the last survivor of a people now dead.

There is blood everywhere. Nothing else glints on the surface. The hopscotch spot, where children played once, is nowhere to be seen. The deep footsteps of people waiting for flour have been erased, along with those who made them. The camp as we know it no longer exists. A hellscape now sits in its place. It's more of a moonscape, to judge from the moonlike ruins. All the cries and lamentations, all the bustle of life and death, and all the human sounds that once filled this place have eerily vanished. Only the birds are singing.

Heedless of my wounds, with whatever might be left in me, I lend a hand to the rescuers. Luckily, the bodies are light to lift, having dwindled to mere skin and bones. Those of the children are almost weightless, as if resting in outer space, or floating on the moon. With little wind, they could float in the air and rise to heaven without a miracle. I see them all, the thin-boned children who died dreaming of the bread that never did come. The hapless fathers and mothers who watched their children perish slowly before their eyes. Their souls must be in heaven right now. Or so we believe, for it would be inhumane to believe otherwise. At long last, I see her, the beautiful girl with the olive eyes, freckled face, and a body thinned out by hunger. There she lies on the ground, with nothing left of her in this sad world, save for an empty bowl and a handful of red flour.

The Flour Massacre, which occurred on February 29, 2024, was one in a long series of horrific massacres carried out during the Gaza Genocide. The victims were among thousands of forcibly starved Palestinians in Gaza who died craving a last meal on this Earth.

This book is dedicated to their memory.

About the Author

Seraj Assi was born and raised in Palestine. He holds a PhD in Arabic Studies from Georgetown University. In addition to *Red Flour,* he is the author of *Rubble* (PM Press) and *My Life as an Alien* (Tartarus Press). His academic publications include *The History and Politics of the Bedouin* (Routledge 2018). He writes for numerous outlets, including *Jacobin Magazine, Truthout, Common Dreams,* among others. He teaches Palestinian Literature at American University in Washington, DC. He lives in Washington, DC.

About Common Notions

Common Notions is a publishing house and programming platform that fosters new formulations of living autonomy. We aim to circulate timely reflections, clear critiques, and inspiring strategies that amplify movements for social justice.

Our publications trace a constellation of critical and visionary meditations on the organization of freedom. By any media necessary, we seek to nourish the imagination and generalize common notions about the creation of other worlds beyond state and capital. Inspired by various traditions of autonomism and liberation—in the US and internationally, historical and emerging from contemporary movements—our publications provide resources for a collective reading of struggles past, present, and to come.

Common Notions regularly collaborates with political collectives, militant authors, radical presses, and maverick designers around the world. Our political and aesthetic pursuits are dreamed and realized with Antumbra Designs.

www.commonnotions.org
info@commonnotions.org

COMMON NOTIONS

Become A Common Notion Monthly Sustainer

These are decisive times ripe with challenges and possibility, heartache, and beautiful inspiration. More than ever, we need timely reflections, clear critiques, and inspiring strategies that can help movements for social justice grow and transform society.

Help us amplify those words, deeds, and dreams that our liberation movements, and our worlds, so urgently need.

Movements are sustained by people like you, whose fugitive words, deeds, and dreams bend against the world of domination and exploitation.

For collective imagination, dedicated practices of love and study, and organized acts of freedom. By any media necessary. With your love and support.

Monthly sustainers start at $15 and receive each new book in our publishing program.

commonnotions.org/sustain